T0168588

ALEJANDRO AND THE
FISHERMEN OF TANCAY

Camino del Sol

A Latina and Latino Literary Series

Alejandro and the Fishermen of Tancay

Braulio Muñoz

Translated from the Spanish by Nancy K. Muñoz

The University of Arizona Press

Tucson

The University of Arizona Press
© 2008 Braulio Muñoz
All rights reserved

Library of Congress Cataloging-in-Publication Data

Muñoz, Braulio, 1946–
 [Alejandro y los pescadores de Tancay. English]
 Alejandro and the fishermen of Tancay / Braulio
Muñoz ; translated from the Spanish by Nancy K.
Muñoz
     p. cm. — (Camino del sol)
  ISBN 978-0-8165-2679-6 (pbk.)
  I. Muñoz, Nancy K. II. Title.
PQ7079.M86A4413   2008
863'.7—dc22   2007047750

Manufactured in the United States of America on
acid-free, archival-quality paper.

13   12   11   10   6   5   4   3   2

In memory of Julián Elías
and for the fishermen of Tancay

Translator's Preface

Chimbote, where our story is set, is a port located on the northeast Pacific coast of Peru about two hundred miles north of Lima, the capital. Chimbote Bay once had such beautiful blue waters and clean sandy beaches that it was called the Pearl of the Pacific. Chimbote Bay sits on a particularly dry expanse of the northern Peruvian desert at the foothills of the Andes and is connected to the Santa Valley through the small Lacramarca River. Villa María, the neighborhood where much of the action of our story takes place, is located a mile south of the center of Chimbote. The little mountain called Tancay, where the rock fishermen in our story used to fish, is located some five miles south of Villa María.

The earliest inhabitants in the area were the Yungas. These pre-Columbian people were the first to use reed boats and brown cotton nets to catch an extensive variety of fish. The arrival of new peoples such as the Mochicas and the Chimú did not substantially change the region's ecology. Chimbote Bay continued to be the source of a varied diet for its rather small population. The coming of the Spanish conquerors in the sixteenth century did not change the bay's character dramatically. Neither did the building of the Chimbote -Huallanca railroad in 1871, nor the laying of the Pan American Highway in 1930. As late as 1940, the estimated population of Chimbote had reached only about 4,200 inhabitants.

The dramatic transformation of the bay began with the building of a dam up in the Andes to supply hydroelectric power for Chimbote's steel mill, the first in Peru, built in 1943. Immigrants from all over the country, but particularly from the northern highlands, began arriving in ever larger numbers to work on these new projects. This incipient development was soon followed by the rapid growth of the fish-meal industry in the next decade. If by 1950 Chimbote had an estimated population of 15,600, by 1960 it had 63,970 inhabitants, and by 1981 its population had almost quadrupled to 213,313. The current estimates approach the half-million mark.

Since the 1960s, Peru has been the foremost producer of fish meal. This is obtained by catching anchoveta in large vessels and transporting them to factories where they are boiled down in large ovens to separate the fish meal from water and fish oils. Because of this industry's rapid growth and bad urban planning, about 70 percent of these factories are located in residential neighborhoods. When the factories are burning at full capacity, the odor of boiled fish makes the air almost unbreathable. And the discharge of unprocessed industrial and residential waste directly into the bay has made Chimbote, once the Pearl of the Pacific, the third most polluted city in Peru.

In addition to these man-made catastrophes, Chimbote has suffered its quota of natural disasters. In 1970, it was very near the epicenter of the great earthquake that shook Peru, killing some 70,000 people in the affected area but particularly in the highlands. The port itself was devastated. Two years later the Lacramarca River inundated the city, which did not dry out for several weeks. Another flood and tidal wave occurred in 1983.

As a port engulfed in rapid and unplanned growth, Chimbote has been strongly affected by the sociopolitical developments in Peru over the past half-century. It has thus also suffered the waves of violent political repressions that have marked the country's history. Consequently, the people of Chimbote have had to mourn the deaths of many citizens who have now and again spoken out against oppression. In 1960, for example, the police killed four workers at the steel mill for demanding higher wages. In 1971, a student was killed, but his body "disappeared." The appalled population demanded that the government give it back. After several days of protest on the streets, the police returned the body, which had been buried in a neighboring town in an unmarked grave. In 1973, two union leaders were assassinated for organizing workers.

It is within this historical context that the people of Chimbote experienced the terror-filled days of the 1980s when, because of the terror tactics used by the Shining Path guerrillas and the government, some 68,000 people were killed or "disappeared."

Alejandro and the Fishermen of Tancay has these historical developments as a backdrop. The bulk of the novel reflects the experiences of the people of Tancay in the years between 1960 and 1990, but, of course, it is not an ethnography, although the author spent more than twenty years, on and off, living and fishing among the rock fishermen of Tancay. Nor is it meant as a historical account, although the outlines of Chimbote's history and some of its important historical personalities are clearly visible. Finally, it is not an analysis of the sociopolitical events that have taken place over the past century in this once beautiful place. *Alejandro and the Fishermen of Tancay* is a novel and, most of all, is meant as an offering of memory for the people of Chimbote.

Nancy K. Muñoz

Alejandro and the Fishermen of Tancay

1
The Valley

Look at that beautiful sky, Alejandro: With which star do we begin to unravel the mystery of its nature, of its way of being? It is difficult to see where this light is born, so blue and so cold inside us. . . . That is how memories are, too . . . difficult to grasp the sense of their nature, of their way of being. So where do we begin to remember what happened? . . . Sometimes it is painful to relive misfortunes. . . . But let us remember together, Alejandro. So that you can find your *sitio*, your place. So you may go in peace and return one day to dance with the sun. But please do not be impatient upon hearing my voice. Do not say, "Don Morales leaves out too much." Because to remember is always at the same time to forget.

The desert is like a narrow ribbon. It is like a snake lying between cold waters and hot mountains. The yellow sand, almost blue when the air is misty, turns the desert hard, desolate. But, even so, many people have frolicked and suffered there since the beginning of time. Many cultures, as they say, have come and gone among those black rocks, those slow dunes, and those once free-flowing rivers. One can see them in the ruins discovered by people who come up from Lima.

They say that the Moche arrived first. But maybe there were others. Because one never knows. The Moche lived around Santa, to the north. They were good farmers, they say. I think they lived by fishing; people from Santa were good with the sea before they became peons. It was from there that people began to fish with *caballitos de totora*, rush boats, and brown cotton nets.

But then came the Chimú. People from even farther north.

I

People who liked to live in cities built of mud. I have visited Chan Chan, just beyond Trujillo. Those cities must have been big. There must have been temples, warehouses, planting fields there. Because the Chimú were good at making cities. Their gods must have been strong and very demanding. But in the end it did not help them at all to enclose themselves behind mud walls because the Incas came and destroyed everything.

The Incas were extending their kingdom all the way to Ecuador. They say it was because the Inca king wanted to marry the queen of Quito. Who knows? The thing is that the Incas surrounded Chan Chan. They must have sat there like clay statues surrounding the walled city, with their llamas and guanacos. People say that they sat there for twelve years, until, at last, tired, abandoned by their demanding gods, the Chimú left their labyrinths to surrender to Waina Capac, the most ferocious of all the Incas. Because they say that the Incas were ferocious in those times.

But the Incas did not last long as rulers in these lands. They had just settled in when the Spaniards arrived. The Spaniards came in sailing ships, they say. Big vessels like floating houses, full of rats. They must have barely made it. They must have come with the bad wind. Once here, they went to Cajamarca and captured the Inca Atahualpa, the crafty one who had defeated Huascar, his brother. The Spaniards ravaged everything: temples, farms, women, until they were satiated. That is how we came to be.

So many things must have happened since then. All these lands became haciendas, farms, ranches. Even the desert came to be owned. Yes, so many things must have happened! When war came to Europe, as they call it, these lands were almost dead. A little bit of cotton, a few fish, nothing more. Most of the people had gone away by now. Only peons remained. Nobody fished anymore. The port became a place for rich folk who came from Lima, from Chile, from Ecuador, to spend their honeymoon. That is when they built the Hotel Chimú. That is why it has always been pink. To please the newlyweds. The Moche, the Chimú, began working there, all dressed up in uniforms.

The steel mill came later. The president said that he wanted to build a Peruvian Pittsburgh. . . . I wonder what that is? . . . He sent his engineers to dam the River Santa upstream, in the gray mountains. They say he made a lake so big that from then on all the rainbows from around here ended in the middle of it. From that lake now spring several small rivers. That is how they wanted to stop the desert that was about to bury the valley. Because that is how the desert is. If you leave it alone, it will cover everything, little by little, like sleep.

In those days they also built the damn factories. Just for exporting. To feed pigs and cows in other lands. But, despite everything, people came here like flies. By the '60s, when we first met, there were already thousands upon thousands of souls, about a quarter of a million. Do you remember? They came from everywhere. From the highlands, from the desert, from the *barriadas*, the shantytowns, of Lima, even from the jungle. Everybody wanted to start a business. Everybody wanted to be a fisherman. If only it could have been so! In the end most of them contented themselves with working in the damn factories. Some ended up as prostitutes, and others became pimps in La Casa Rosada.

So many foreigners came, Alejandro, that there arose a tangled web of languages everywhere. Black people and white people went about speaking as if only for themselves. But the gringos, the fair-skinned folk, spread farther. Do you remember? Father Parker came to build the Mundo Mejor school. Sister Josefa began setting up medical outposts. The poor thing walked around the desert like a *duende*, a sprite, with white wings. The Peace Corps volunteers helped to build bridges and taught people how to swim. The gringos gave us so much and took so much from us in the years they stayed among us that we must remember them too, Alejandro. . . .

2

Chimbote

How does one unravel the mystery of the nature of things, of their way of being? . . . Some people say that one can read the future in the wrinkles of old folks. That all you have to do is concentrate. I think that you can read there, if at all, only what remains of the past—what can no longer be changed, but only remembered. Look at my hands. See? Knotty. Bony. Flaccid. It is only from so much living. No, Alejandro. The future does not leave traces. . . . But now it is not about me. What we have to remember is for you.

In the '60s, Chimbote was a city on the move. There was only one traffic light and the Pan American Highway was the only paved road. The other streets were dusty, full of potholes, and lined with open bars. People were rowdy and fought at the drop of a hat. But, above all, we have to remember the smell. The sticky, greenish smell of boiled fish. When the wind was not blowing, a cloak of gray mist, vomited from the damn factories, crept through the streets. Remember?

There was not much room to live. People found places in the cramped alleyways as best they could. Without water, without electricity, without anything. Tiny places where nothing would fit but a bed and a kerosene stove. Not even a table or anything. That is why the police could not stop the growth of the barriadas. They sprouted up everywhere, as if from out of nowhere, and in time they crawled halfway up the surrounding gray mountains.

But, of course, it only seemed like they came from out of nowhere. Because people sometimes made plans for whole months. They would buy their reed mats, wires, poles, and string. They would even make a Peruvian flag. When they were ready, they would look for a place on the outskirts of the desert, and there they would invade—almost always on Saturdays, so that the men could help carrying things. "Ready to go, don Morales? Let's go."

Mondays were the most difficult days because the men would go back to work, and then the police would come to destroy what had been built. The women, who always stayed behind with the children and the old folks, had to defend their plots as best they could, with sticks and stones. Many were roughed up and put in jail. There was a lot of suffering in those days. That is why some barriadas did not last. But those that remained were soon reinforced. Within days the reed mats would be replaced with bricks, made by hand in the backyards with sand, cement, and steel molds. Soon, the school would be built. The market would come later.

That is how Villa María was founded, wasn't it? In the beginning there were only about thirty of us. But we prepared for two months. When don Jeremías—the owner of the only *colectivo*, the communal taxicab, in those days—gave us the word, we picked up our things, and off we went to the desert. Quietly. Like shadows. Then don Augusto, who was already with us, divided a swathe of desert into sections. His work lasted until 1970, when the earthquake came, and Villa María was forced to spread south.

Not everything was good in those years, of course. But people had a thirst for life. The port was a whole world of adventures, of opportunities, of dreams. The bad things were seen only as something inevitable in life. People formed trade unions, they built houses, they ate all kinds of foods, and, let us not forget, the theaters played movies all night, and in the movies you could see how other people lived and loved. No, Chimbote was no paradise, but it was better than many other places. I suppose. That is why people came from everywhere bringing their customs along.

But then came the truly bad times, in the '70s, when you had already gone—Why did you go, Alejandro? Where? I wonder what you did that they tried to sink you in the well of forgetfulness—But, in any case . . . first the fish became scarce. The cold current, they say, left the coast. I think instead that Los Gentiles, the gods of our forebears, got angry because we took so much from the sea. . . . The thing is that the port ended up half dead. On top of that, there came a strong earthquake, and that was followed by a tidal wave. All of Chimbote was filled with salt water. People had to walk around carrying their shoes for weeks. And then, to top it all off, when things were beginning to dry out, there came the *huaico*, a mudslide. They say that water and mud came tumbling down from the gray mountains because Los Gentiles got tired of seeing all the rainbows in the same place. Who knows? . . . The fact is that many people were buried alive.

Looking at things from far away, as always, the rich decided to take everything away with them. Maybe that is why the government nationalized the fishing industry. But, as usual, the government did not solve anything either. A year after the earthquake people were still ambling about without work, kicking stones. There were fights in Lima. Petitions. Strikes. Until some generals got the idea of deposing those in power. Bam! Another government. Now they started giving the factories back to the rich. Maybe that is why the fishermen got angry. Maybe they were afraid of losing everything. They organized. They protested. But all of that only worsened their suffering. The government accused them of being Communists and called in the troops. The fisherman and their wives holed up in the union hall, ready to fight. For what! The troops attacked the place and took everyone to the garrison. Genaro swears in anger that there was a bloody reprisal that day. It is a bitter memory, Alejandro. . . .

3
The Fishermen

Everyone thinks that the fishermen go out early and come back late with their boats full of fish. They see them as quiet folks on the sea, always looking off into the distance, wishing to return home. That is what you thought, even after you came back, secretly, in 1985. Don't you remember? And mostly that is how they are, Alejandro. Extremely generous, full of dreams, spendthrifts, rowdy on land, strong and steady men in defending their cause . . . because, to tell the truth, a fisherman will die for his rights. . . . So, all things considered, it's good to be a fisherman on the high seas, as they say.

But those of us who fished on the rocks were not like that. We were solitary, patient, immersed in the shadows of the rocks and the sound of the sea. We would lose ourselves in the labyrinths of Tancay for entire days, watching the water, white and alive, pounding against the Andes. In summer we would go out bare-chested. In winter we would wrap ourselves in the ocean mist. Looking inward, following our thoughts, we would let ourselves be taken away by the currents flowing through the seaweed.

We did not need fishing rods, like in those places you told us about. We had to let the hooks drop in the swirling waters, and for that we needed our hands. We had to feel the turbulence between our fingers. Perhaps these wrinkles on my hands are the remnants of all that. Traces of what once was, of what we once were. . . . No, Alejandro, fishing rods would not work around here. . . . But let us remember everything with patience. From the beginning. We have time. Doña Pelagia will send us word.

When the people of Santa fished, they did it with cotton lines.

9

But those lines are no longer used. I have always used nylon. Only very heavy and very light when I began. Of all colors and thicknesses in the last days. The Germans, as they are called, make good fishing lines. There is a brand, "Payaso," that lasts a long time against the wind. Is that perhaps the only good thing that has come from abroad, like Genaro used to say?

Whatever line you used, you had to twirl it around and around in the air before casting it. It was necessary to aim well to hit the right spot. And all that twirling ended up twisting the line. So you had to stop fishing to untwist it from time to time; otherwise, it would get snarled up into a ball. You had to know when to spread it out, untwist it, and roll it back up. That is why the Good Fisherman knew when to stop fishing, even if the fish were biting everywhere; it was so he would not lose his line in the wind. The Good Fisherman did not just go on and on; he always controlled his desires. That is something I think you never learned, Alejandro. Pity. Look what that has brought us. . . .

There were different kinds of hooks. Some were this little and some this big. We changed hooks according to the color of the foam, the movement of the sea, the level of the tide, the flight of the birds, the path of the sun, the fish we wanted. Because the Good Fisherman did not covet the fish that others were catching. No. He had to decide. This one today. That one tomorrow. He had to be patient. Patience is something one learns, Alejandro; it grows out of our sense of time: there are no holes there, no escape. Time is like a ribbon coiled up inside us. Each of us has one of its own length . . . but let us leave that for later. . . .

The largest hooks were used without bait. They were very special; not all of us could use them because it is not easy to be a *rosetero*. We would tie four large hooks in the form of a rose, like this, and attach them to a heavy line. Just like that, we would twirl it around and around to one side, until casting it to the foam. We would then begin pulling it in slowly, feeling the brushing of the thick seaweed, the floating snails, the small fish, then we would pull hard and catch the prey. Not many of us could fish like that, without bait. When you came back, you had much yet to learn. Perhaps you would never have learned.

The baits were also very different. There were all kinds. It depended in part on what fish you wanted to catch, in part on the cravings of the fish themselves—because, as with people, the crafty fish liked to vary their tastes. They even took turns. One could catch different types of fish from the same spot, depending on the bait. But sometimes the sea would affect them. Whenever the sea was sick, when it turned red in the evening and had white foam at dawn, then the fish would not even eat. That is how it was.

The best bait was langostino, that little pink crustacean that lived in little holes at the water's edge. When we first met—When was that, Alejandro, in '66?—there were a lot of langostinos at Veintisiete de Octubre. I used to walk along those beaches early in the morning, looking for them. It was so cold! But it was worth it. There I would go, searching, searching for the langostinos' little bubbles. . . . The langostinos disappeared, along with the *cochos*, the brown pelicans, when the damn factories began to vomit into the sea.

4
The Coasts

In my head, deep inside me, our coast has two parts that come together at El Dorado, that blue mountain with the white cloud that looks far out to the sea. Each part has its own way of being. The part closer to us begins at Veintisiete de Octubre. It has freshwater, flowers, marshes that extend all the way to El Dorado. Before the president got the idea of building a Pittsburgh, there was everything there: sea lions, ducks, snakes, even penguins. The few people who remained in the area walked along those beaches, looking for treasures brought from the high seas by the cold currents.

When I arrived here, the beaches of El Dorado were still clean. The women would gather seaweed in little straw baskets, and the men would look for hairy crabs. The young boys would bask in the sun for a long time before plunging into the cold waters to get mussels and snails. Don Tico, the man who taught me how to fish, said that there were big octopuses. People cautioned against Los Duendes, who in those days still walked around looking for someone to play with.

By the '70s, the damn factories had gotten hold of everything. The beaches turned black and muddy. The poor little animals were drowned with the vomit that came into the bay. By the '80s, when you came to visit us dressed like a woman, all that was left were a few ghost crabs burying the dead fish. The people did not go there anymore. Even the beaches of El Dorado were full of *aguaje*, that contaminated, soupy, greenish sludge.

Some time ago—I tell you this as an example—the people who fished at La Playa del Viento, in El Dorado, found thousands of drunken fish. The fish were just floating around, not afraid of anything. They even let themselves be caught with bare hands. The fishermen gave thanks to the sea and brought back all the fish they could. They sold them right away. They bought little things for their children. They were as happy as could be. But the next day they heard that the people had gotten sick, that many of them were walking around drunk, bumping into things. Some ended up in the hospital. . . . Then came the news that they had eaten poisoned fish. And it was then that the fishermen realized that those fish had not been intoxicated by Los Gentiles or by the sea, but by the damn factories. From then on they learned never to eat drunken fish who let themselves be caught with bare hands. . . .

Between El Dorado and Tancay, which is where we met, there is La Playa Desierta, a long deserted beach. If you still remember, you know that from there you can see Tancay, a stout little mountain in the middle of the other part of our coast. It is a long, long walk along that beach. Until recently, you could catch *pampanito*, butterfish, at El Pozo, near the end of La Playa Desierta. But now there is nothing left. So you keep walking and walking—until you can see the first rocks of Tancay, all covered with black mussels. Sometimes there were fish there. But mostly that was the reign of *los cangrejeros*, the crabbers. They have their stories. Don't you agree? We have to remember them, too. They do teach us something.

Some years ago two crabbers caught so many crabs from those rocks that they filled two enormous sacks. The sacks were so big that they could not carry both at the same time to the Pan American Highway. So they carried one and left the other behind, hidden. Someone must have seen them. Someone must have waited until they were far away because when they returned, the sack had disappeared. "Who took our sack, don Morales?" they asked me the next day. "Who knows?" I told them. "Maybe other crabbers." They believed me because everyone knew that crabbers could not be trusted. But I thought that Los Gentiles had gotten angry. They must have thought that the crabbers had become too greedy. You never know. In those days Los Gentiles could still see into our hearts.

Beyond the reign of the crabbers lies La Pared, the wall. It is about a hundred meters high and looks out to where the sun sets.

There was good fishing there. But only the best fishermen would dare to fish on La Pared. There are so many stories of danger and death, so many frightful moments smeared on those bare rocks. . . . You get to the middle of La Pared by way of a very narrow path, not even half a meter wide. There is barely a spot to stand and drop your line. In summer the hot wind blows everywhere. In winter things get even worse. The sun beats down so hard it leaves you blind. That is why we never let you go up there, Alejandro. You could have fallen. Because you always went around with your head in the clouds. . . .

Most of us fished from La Mesa, a flat rock, or on La Punta, a cluster of slippery rocks protruding from the middle of Tancay. We had to pick a spot according to the tide, the sun, the type of fish we wanted to catch. La Mesa was good for pampanito. If you wanted *chita*, grunt fish, you had to go out to La Punta. If you were content with *tramboyo*, blenny, you could spend the day in spots with gentle whirlpools. A place for everyone. Because that is how it is, Alejandro; everything has its own nature, its own way of being. . . . But let us go on remembering.

You must remember that by the late '60s a summer camp for children was built on the south side of Tancay. Naturally, we did not like it at all. But what could we do? Nothing. At first we had hopes that, as with many things that came from the city, the camp would not last. But, instead, it became permanent. The mayor even posted a watchman. The poor man came to live there with his three dogs and two cats. All alone. His name was Arturo, and he liked to drink. God knows why he sought a job that brought out his awful loneliness. The thing is that he managed there as best he could. . . . Once he got so drunk that his spirit began to wander in the desert. You could see that absence in his eyes. We found him surrounded by ghost crabs that were already trying to bury him. He did not want to move. We had to carry him from there, tie him to his bed, and give him only seaweed to eat for five days, until his spirit returned.

When you came to visit us dressed like a woman, back in '85, the reed-mat huts of the camp had been replaced by several train coaches. Do you remember? They appeared one day, as if from nowhere. Chochita, who is not known for inventing stories, told me that he had heard that the coaches had come all the way from San Francisco, a place beyond Mexico, as they call it. But doña Pelagia says they did not come from that far away. She says that those coaches were from the train that used to carry people from Chimbote to the Callejon de Huaylas, a beautiful valley in the highlands that was destroyed by Los Gentiles shortly after the earthquake because it was attracting too many tourists. . . .

Farther south of the camp there is a peaceful beach. In the middle of it, about fifty meters offshore, there are two large rocks called Las Dos Hermanas, the Two Sisters. Those rocks have given us much and taken much from us. The few who dared to fish there would dig small hollows on the beach, just behind the low mounds of sand. There they would wait for low tide. When it was time, they would tie themselves to each other with a heavy rope and swim to the rocks. They would climb up to the first sister, round the top, and jump to the second sister over a short breach. Those rocks were slimy and slippery, and they concealed treacherous waters. People have died there. I will tell you later what happened to Hermelindo. . . .

Beyond Las Dos Hermanas, still to the south, there is a large rocky mound called La Cocina, the Kitchen. Genaro says that a while back, there were ovens there. To extract the blubber from sea lions. It must be true because when I first set foot on those rocks, there was still an odor of scorched meat. . . . Just beyond that is Besique, a cove that once had a little train and everything. You have to enter there through a tunnel . . . but you know that, Alejandro. You knew that world. Before you got involved in fighting for us. But you are so silent on this cold, blue night. . . .

I will go on with the story then, as though you did not know. But listen; keep those sights and sounds as provision against loneliness. . . . The tunnel is wide; it used to be part of a railroad line that, up until the '60s, carried cotton and sugar to the cove. You must remember the train, even though in those days you had eyes and ears only for politics. Big black men carried sacks of sugar and cotton on their backs. They ran over the loose boards of the pier out to the small boats that would come and go. Because the big ships waited farther out. It was beautiful to watch them work. They sang. They laughed. But all of that ended. Now Besique is only for summer vacationers. If you could see it! They have repaired the

Pan American Highway. Restaurants and bars everywhere. Where before there were stingrays and sharks, now there are only tourists.

There is not much to say about places farther south, Alejandro. El Patillo Ahogado, the Drowned Duckling, is there, far away, amid small beaches with black rocks scattered all over the place. You learn a lot fishing there, though. That was where Lalo learned to think like a tramboyo, for example. I will tell you about that later, too. Because when Lalo learned how to follow the tramboyo in its labyrinths, you were no longer here. . . . Beyond that is Samanco. That world I do not know very well. Why lie to you?

The Pan American Highway was a frontier. It was stretched out in the desert like a thin black thread. Brilliant under the sun. When the wind that comes down from the highlands would blow strong, we could hear the trailer trucks running like deer across those sands. It would not have occurred to anyone of us to go into the desert beyond the thin black thread. In 1985, when you came to visit us, half scared, with your flowered dress—What had you done, I wonder?—people were saying that the government wanted to make those desolate places flower. I thought that would never happen. On those yellow sands, I told myself, Los Gentiles are waiting to make war. But it seems that Los Gentiles have decided to retreat even deeper into the desert. Let us hope they will soon take a stand and let the ruckus begin.

5

On the Fringes of Tancay

That is how it was, Alejandro. Before the sludge, the waters of Tancay were teeming with fish. There was a wide variety and enough for everyone. There were even those fish who rarely come to the rocks, and if they do, they do not come to eat. They would come mostly when the mist licked the cliffs, as the sun was rising. To catch them, you had to use boat and net. And for that there were the *bolicheros*, the net fishermen. . . . Let us remember from the beginning all the different kinds of men who left their footprints on Tancay. What do you say, Alejandro? Without sadness, but with warmth in our hearts, so that one day they, too, can return to those rocks and deserts to find their sitios and dance with the sun.

The bolicheros came often to Tancay. They would cross the desert in an old pickup truck, carrying a boat and lots of nets. They would park the truck somewhere, open the railings, lower the boat to the sand, and fill it with ropes, nets, and oars. Six or seven men would then line up on both sides of the boat, lift it up over their heads, and cross the sands in a single dash. They looked like those men you see in the movies dressed like angels. Except that they were dark-skinned, like us.

Once in the water, two of the bolicheros would row out to where the birds were circling. At times they would seem to disappear between the swelling of the waves. But they would always manage to spread their nets in wide circles and return to the shore holding the ends. Then came the best part. They had to pull against the sea. But, believe it or not, laughing and swearing, the poor guys would bring in their fish. Many times. From a distance, they seemed to be floating on air. It was beautiful to watch them work.

But, to be honest, the bolicheros did not belong to Tancay. They went around everywhere together in a group and hardly ever talked to us. And the truth is, too, that we felt sorry for them. They were like peons. Or, worse, like the workers in the damn factories. They would work their hearts out for the owner, a fat man who would stay behind sitting in the truck. So, all things considered, it was not good to be a bolichero.

But listen, there was one man with a boat who was really good. You must have seen him because when the sludge was doing away with everything, he kept coming. He could certainly have belonged among us; he could even have become a Good Fisherman. Genaro even says that he already was. But, as for me, I believe he was a solitary man. Because there are men like that, Alejandro. They search for and love the silence inside them—which is not like this silence, one of remembering with you, which I do not like and at times even makes me want to cry. . . .

He arrived shortly after you left, after the earthquake. He came with his straw hat pulled down to his eyes and his caballito de totora over his head. Squatting on the beach, he looked like one of those *huacos*, the ancient pottery figures in the form of men, that doña Pelagia collects. He sat thinking, looking at the ocean as if he were seeing it for the first time. He left his caballito de totora on the sand and went back the same way he had come. We went to see the contraption. It was as light as paper. Sheer straw! The next morning, when we arrived, the man was already in his boat, out in the ocean, catching chita. But he never came near to where we were. He knew how to show respect.

Who knows what his name was. But I am sure he needed solitude, silence. To fish. To live. Genaro spoke with him several times. He told me that the man never felt alone. Rather, he had patience. Because, at times, words are superfluous, Alejandro, when they make the spirit overflow. Not like now, when it is better to go on remembering in order to gather the spirit scattered by misfortune. . . . I never saw him again. Maybe he is fishing up north, where he must have come from. Maybe he is with El Rey de la Mojarrilla, the King of the Croaker, watching us from afar, laughing at us. . . .

The *marucheros* were something else. They searched everywhere for *maruchas*, those little shellfish that look like the giant corn kernels from the highlands. They had a nose for them. Are you listening, Alejandro? Do not go and lose the thread of remembrance. I do not want to remember with you all over again. . . . They always came at low tide, be it early or late. They would bring several sacks and their *caitos*, those tools with iron teeth and a net for a tail. Rarely would there be more than three of them, although there were eventually around ten of them just before the sludge came.

They would sit on the shore, all in a line, to wait for the tide to go out. It seemed like the world of the rocks did not interest them. When low tide came, they would begin: with their fingers laced overhead, they would bend to touch their ankles, their backs, their necks, their butts. They looked liked those Andean dancers who dance with scissors at the feast of San Pedro. In summer, against the setting sun, the marucheros looked like golden birds with long legs.

They went into the water in one dash and planted their caitos in the sand as the waves retreated. When the waves returned, they would straighten up to wash the trapped maruchas. When they finally had enough, they came out running to the shore and placed the maruchas on cotton blankets. Winter must have been the most difficult time because that is when the ocean winds really sweep the beaches. . . . And they were naked. Imagine that. . . . After a while, the marucheros would put on their clothes and leave with their sacks on their shoulders.

They did form part of our world. They told us about other beaches and traded us maruchas for fish. Sometimes we helped them carry their loads to the Pan American Highway. Even so, they always lived on the fringes. They never became like us. And with reason. The poor guys had to get wet and carry heavy loads in order to make a living—things that a fisherman would never do. The *chiteros*, those who catch chita, said that the poor marucheros had to chew coca in order live that way. They looked at them with disdain. As for me, I think we never got to know them. We saw them only from a distance. And at a distance people and things appear strange. What do you say, Alejandro?

The crabbers were closer to us. When you arrived for the first time, before you got tangled up with bullets and death, there were about thirty crabbers on the beaches. They gathered seaweed, mussels, snails, crabs, and octopuses. Some hunted ducks with a slingshot. But few remained after the earthquake. The sludge began to kill everything: first, the crabbers abandoned Veintisiete de Octubre; later, they had to abandon El Dorado. When you visited us in 1985, you must remember, they would go only to Tancay, Besique, and La Cocina. Now they no longer exist. They have been lost.

They used to work all around us. They were in the way and got into everything. We had to be careful not to hit them in the head with our lead sinkers. But they helped us to free our hooks from the rocks, they warned us when a big wave was coming, they would give us sea worms as bait. We knew all their names. Sometimes they even sat with us at lunchtime. I had friends among them. But, still and all, they never became Good Fishermen. They got wet. They got cut. They crawled on the rocks. The Good Fisherman never gets wet, never runs, never crawls.

6
The Night Fishermen

When you came for the first time, there were several *mojarrilleros*, those who fished for croakers in Tancay, although most likely you did not see them. You never had eyes for them. It seems your compassion was already far away, among strangers. But we must remember them, Alejandro. We must follow the thread of remembrance and recall not only what you saw and felt, but also what others saw and felt for you or with you. For, as Genaro says, we all become what we are or were by the fault or the good will of others.
. . .

Most of the mojarrilleros fished from the pier at Besique. They would tie about seven hooks on a heavy line and pull in mojarrillas like they were bunches of grapes. In a short time they would have enough to eat and to sell. But, for that very reason, the mojarrilleros never became Good Fishermen. Because the Good Fisherman does not live by a fish that catches itself. Although you may laugh.

The Good Fisherman would catch that little fish that croaks like a frog only so as not to go home empty-handed. And he had to do it on the sly because the others would make fun of him: "Ah, you brought only your shoelaces today, huh?" they would say. Because even the tourists could catch mojarrillas. They would come with their radios, their balls, their bottles of beer, and still catch mojarrillas. Sometimes one of the fishermen would fill sacks of mojarrillas and try to sneak up to the Pan American Highway. There the blessed mojarrillas would get their revenge. They would be croaking out loud the whole way.

But we must remember that among the mojarrilleros in those

23

times there was also El Rey. Back then he was seen only as an older man who always went around with his son, a boy who eventually became a famous *rocanrolero*, rock-and-roll singer. But, as is also happening with you, El Rey eventually sank deep into the souls of all who knew him. You knew him, too, although you probably do not remember him. Back then El Rey had not yet become what he would eventually be. He was just a mojarrillero.

Most of the fishermen went to Tancay at dawn and returned home when the sun had already set behind El Dorado. But there were some, *los nocturnos*, who worked only at night. People that we hardly knew. They were very solitary. Maybe it was because they risked their lives among the shadows, the waves, and the sounds. They waited for nightfall behind the mounds of sand where they had made their shelter with driftwood, *juncos*, and seaweed. They chewed coca, drank black coffee, and smoked Inca cigarettes. Hardy men.

Genaro used to walk with them. He wasn't as he might appear now. He says that los nocturnos were like everybody else. They talked about their children, about the feast of San Pedro, about their joys and their sorrows. They would wait for low tide, listening to the silence, until the shadows became soft, round, like the humming of the desert. They would then stand up, put on their cotton belts, rub their hands and legs, throw their sacks over their shoulders and head for the fishing spots. They moved like Las Almitas, the spirits. When the moon was full, their shirts of cotton covered with fish scales would glow. They hardly ever talked then. On a very dark night they could be found only by the light of their cigarettes.

Los nocturnos knew how to catch chita. They had patience. They were steadfast in body and soul. But, even with all that, only Genaro was ever considered a Good Fisherman. He would laugh at us daytime fishermen, saying that we were missing the marrow of life, that there was nothing more beautiful than to catch chita at night. In truth, we fishermen did not appreciate los nocturnos. We would say that they had to sleep in the sand, near the ghost crabs, those who bury the dead; that their teeth were green from chewing so much coca; that their eyes were glassy from looking so much into the night; that they were always dazed from not sleeping like everyone else.

One looks at people from the outside and says, "This is how they must be, this is how they are." But, in truth, no one ever really knows anything about anyone else. Los nocturnos could have fished at any hour of the day. The thing is that they felt at home in the silence. "We like the night," Genaro told me when we first met, so long ago now. "It's serene. We like the moon most of all. Our mother, they say. Too much noise, people, in the daytime. The night is peaceful. We are all alone. . . . " He took me with him several times. It was really dangerous. There were many temptations. Los Gentiles come out at those hours to roam the beaches and traverse time. . . . But it is beautiful to listen to the deep sounds of the ocean that are heightened with the moon.

The *cordeleros* fished with line on the beaches. Lalo began like that, and so did you. But you never learned from them. Until it was too late. If only you had wanted to! We would not be like we are now, groping for handles to the past. . . . The cordeleros had special sinkers and a lot of patience. They looked for their spots sensing the water, the foam, the birds. Sometimes they walked for miles. Their footsteps drew out a gentle sound from the wet sand; their words made the wind rejoice. When they found their spot, they set their sacks to one side and concentrated. Words then became superfluous.

A good cordelero would spread his line on the sand. Carefully. Sensing the rhythm of the sea. He would then twirl the sinker over his head, waiting, waiting for the right wave. When the right wave came, he would follow it in, without fear. From there he would let the line fly—near, far, or in between. He would then run back quickly and stand at the water's edge, with the line held lightly between his fingers, with his gaze turned inward. . . . The cordelero's sinker looked like a spider. It had little wire feet to hold onto the ocean floor. That is why it did not move. And a good cordelero never brought the line in with bait still on it unless he wanted to move to another spot. He felt the light touch of the fish, the crosscurrents, the rhythm of the wind. He had a clean heart. Do you understand, Alejandro? A clean heart. All alone, sensing the distances, the cordelero was patience personified. That is what I wanted to teach you when you first arrived, but you were not open to learning such things then. And now? How do we clean your heart? By retracing our footsteps, perhaps . . .

But, anyway. To a bad past, a good memory. The main thing is that we are here, remembering. . . . And it should be said, too, that most of the fishermen did a bit of everything. Sometimes they got wet for being greedy or impatient. Many times they even caught mojarrillas. They were like everybody else.

We should not forget that there were also fishermen who went to Tancay only from time to time. Some did so because they were too old to stand the winter. Others because they were truck drivers, teachers out of work, even bankrupt merchants. Every time they came back, they would have to go onto the rocks with renewed caution. Because it is always difficult to leave the outside world behind. They would lose their hooks. They would swear. They would spit. They would have to begin all over again. Ah, but they did bring us news, both good and bad. They made us laugh, at times even cry. They remembered you well, after you disappeared from these shores. They said that you were betrayed and mistreated for speaking out against Canchero, against what is corrupt in life. . . . But one should not believe everything one hears, right? Besides, it is all in the past. The only thing left for us now is to smooth time by retracing our footsteps. That is why we are together. . . .

1
The Chiteros

These stars are beginning to give me chills. It is as if someone were watching us to see if we are remembering correctly. If only we were inside, at least . . . but doña Pelagia is very determined: "It is better in the backyard; one remembers better under the sky," she says. The thing is that this chair squeezes my whole body, and the cold gives me muscle cramps. . . . But let us just go on. Duties must be fulfilled, and our desire helps. What do you say?

Those who fished only for chita were called chiteros. They were young, but extremely patient—very good fishermen. They could catch fish where there were none. While others would spread out desperately, they would be looking at the water like hawks. They knew how to read the foam, the whirlpools, the colors on the surface of the water. They could feel the sea inside them.

The chitero could wait for hours to cast his line. When he was ready, he would roll up his pants, unbutton his shirt, and approach the water with his eyes closed in order to better sense the rhythm of the ocean. He went down in a single dash to the rocks that were washed by the waves. He threw his line in close, holding the cork spool between his teeth. He followed the bait, alive, banging, spinning in the whirlpools. He had little time between the breaking waves. But he concentrated intensely. His eyes were immersed in the sea; the world outside the play of the water did not exist.

The chiteros used to go everywhere, until around the time when you returned dressed like a woman—maybe you dressed like that so that they would not be merciless with you. . . . We never knew why, right? You did not want to compromise us, I suppose. But let us go on remembering. The chiteros were true rock fishermen. They never fished from the beaches. They had already learned patience. They would rather have gone home empty-handed than with mojarrilla. When they caught small fish, they threw them back to the sea to go on growing. What a pity that not even those fish were allowed to grow. All on account of people like Canchero. That is how it was, Alejandro. Remember. Canchero knew what was going to happen to you. Because, while he had power, he meddled even in people's dreams.

Well, anyway, I'll go on. Within the group of chiteros there were the roseteros, the ones who could catch fish without bait. They had a *roseta*, as I mentioned before, made with four hooks on a heavy line. Sometimes they had a piece of leather for their hand. But everything was coming to an end. . . . When you came back in '85, there were only three of us roseteros left. Genaro did it at night. He says it is easier then. Chochita would fish with a roseta only on a whim. I only did it just in case—in case I might have to teach someone someday. But now it seems I will never be a teacher again. That is how it goes.

We had to feel the whirlpools, the waves, the sun. We could not let ourselves be distracted by the schools of fish that passed by. We could not be greedy. We threw the roseta way out and started pulling it in very slowly, as I told you. We had to close our eyes so we could feel everything inside, in a single bundle. We had to let the little ones pass. Because the big chitas were very clever. They would hide. They would send the little ones out ahead. You had to feel the chita in your very heart, leaving everything else outside. You could feel the roseta brushing against the mussels, the seaweed, the snails. And you would never let yourself be surprised by the water because if it got you, it could pull you in, or it could smash you against the rocks so hard that you would never forget it. You closed your eyes. You emptied yourself of everything. You presented a clean heart.

I used to think that Lalo was going to learn to fish with a roseta. I thought that there was time. I realize now that I was mistaken. . . . They say there are roseteros in the north, up where El Rey went. They say that Chochita is teaching up north, beyond Trujillo, in a port called Paita. But, who knows? . . . Maybe the fish will return, and Lalo will learn. . . . It is sad what I am telling you. But do not worry too much about us. There are always new things to learn in the world. There is always room for hope. Do not look back with bitterness.

8
The Rock

On the road that goes from the Pan American Highway to Tancay, right at the foot of the stout mountain, there is La Piedra, the Rock. Maybe you have not seen it. Because one has to want to see it. One has to see beyond the hardness, the smoothness of that rock. For anyone else it is just a common, ordinary rock. In reality it is the Blessed Virgin, who used to wait for us, welcome us. But you know that. We told you about it. We showed it to you. Don't you remember? Can't you feel it still? Ay, Alejandro, what will become of you? . . . This piercing cold goes right to my bones. . . . Sometimes it seems doña Pelagia gets carried away. If she were not so mysterious . . . but even she showed it to you. She told you its story.

If one looked at La Piedra when the sun was setting over El Dorado, one could see the Blessed Virgin carrying the baby Jesus on her back. That was a sign of hope for those who had a clean heart because, according to doña Pelagia, she was not happy. She knew we were suffering. She saw us. . . . She has been there since the beginning of time, since before the name of her son was known. Maybe in the beginning no one knew that she was waiting for them, welcoming them. Until we came. She used to warn us of dangers. She was our mother.

When Hermelindo, the gringo of the twins, drowned at Las Dos Hermanas, a long time ago now, the face of La Piedra was wet at dawn the next morning. And it did not dry all day because she had cried all night. She knew. That is why we, the old ones, used to look at her face every time we went to Tancay. To see what she was telling us. . . . The young ones no longer saw La Piedra with the same eyes.

They felt bad inside, as though ashamed. Maybe that is why the disaster came upon us. . . .

But at least those young ones knew enough to listen to our stories. They would be quiet. Not like you when you came back, after you had gone to fight, wanting to pump us about everything, about our pleasures and our sins. You never tired of asking us: "And this, don Morales, what is it for? Why don't you sell the fish directly to restaurants? Who knows Canchero well?" You did not understand anything. You would not learn. You were too bent on having everything explained to you. You would interrupt. You were foolish. Maybe now . . .

One time a fisherman was drinking *chicha*, corn beer, up on the rocks. He drank and drank, forgetting about the danger. La Piedra had to tell him to stop acting stupid, without consideration. . . . It was already almost dark when the miracle occurred. The man was just about to take another swig when he heard a voice that seemed to come from everywhere.

"Don't you have children?" La Piedra asked him.

The man, who of course did not have a clean heart, thought it was another fisherman passing nearby. A joke. But even so, drunk and all, he thought about his three children. He only thought it to himself, though.

"Then why don't you go and give them something to eat instead of begging to be taken away to the sitio of the forgotten?"

It was like the voice of a mother. Sweet. Soft. But heard deep inside . . . because La Piedra can read our thoughts. . . . The fisherman got up to see who was talking to him like that. Nothing. Silence. Only gray rocks. That sobered him up. Right then and there he picked up his things and went home. He was scared. When he passed by La Piedra, the fisherman saw the Virgin rocking in the wind. Rocking. Then he understood. Fear turned to gratitude. She had saved his life. He never again drank chicha at Tancay. . . . That is how it was. . . .

Several years ago now—you must remember it because it was in those days when you would not stop talking about the newspaper. "The newspaper this. The newspaper that. Denunciations, editorials," you used to say. You did not talk about anything else. What good did all that do you? Tell me. Your newspaper disappeared like January rain in the desert. . . . But you must remember that we were very upset. We had left hooks and sinkers aside to climb in and out of dump trucks and trailers. We even ended up gathering as a group. That must have been the first and last time that chiteros, crabbers, mojarrilleros, and marucheros walked together.

We were ready to fight because some rich man wanted to take away La Piedra. Imagine that. He said he wanted to take it to Lima, to a museum. For the history of Peru, he said. To hell with history!

"Without her how are we going to know the good things and the bad things that await us on the rocks?" we told him.

The rich man and his people came on a Sunday morning with a crane and a truck. Like other awful things, they came on the road that was made for the summer camp. When they got to the foot of the stout mountain, where La Piedra is, the truck got stuck in the sand. It could not go any farther. They tried to push it uphill; they hooked it to the crane. Nothing. The truck was stuck. So they drove the crane up the hill. It groaned and rolled a little, and when it was just about to reach La Piedra, it, too, got stuck. After much laboring the people sat down. It was useless to go on. The rich man went back to the city.

That was when we arrived. God knows why we went to Tancay so late that day. And it was even a Sunday. But in any case . . . we saw what the rich man was doing. We argued with his people. We told them to stop such foolishness . . . but we knew very well what was going to happen when the rich man returned. Because his people told us that he had gone to look for help, that he was going to come back with big machines and the police to sweep us aside. That is why we decided to go look for help as well.

We went in dump trucks and trailers everywhere. We talked to the people, to don Franco, who was still teaching in Villa María. We went to see Father Parker, the priest from the Mundo Mejor school. We even began to make Peruvian flags. Maybe then you and we were truly the same, Alejandro: warriors who no longer see any other way.

A week passed, and the truck and the crane were still stuck. The following Sunday the rich man came again with his people. He also brought ten policemen. But the people from Villa María, the teachers, Father Parker, don Franco—all came. Together. Walking. They raised so much dust on the road that when they arrived, they were all coughing, and it took them a long time before they could speak. Everyone spoke. Father Parker spoke oddly: "It is their rock, their inheritance," he said. That is how you wrote it. That is how Lalo read it to me, after everything was over. And we were happy, not knowing that for you that was just the beginning, that you were going to leave these shores and go off as if touched by a ghost in search of justice, as you used to say.

That day we did win. As if by a miracle. The rich man had to take away his crane and his truck empty. La Piedra stayed. She is still there, only now she seems to be wrapped in perpetual mist. She suffers for all of us. You must feel her inside you now. Soothing. She will guide you, Alejandro.

9
Patón

The people who knew you are arriving now, Alejandro. Doña Pelagia will receive them and accept their offerings. You never imagined how many friends you had, did you? They truly like you . . . but let them wait for now. . . . Look at the stars. They keep blinking. They seem to want to speak. . . . Do not worry. Doña Pelagia will take care of your friends. Although she must be asking herself why we are taking so long remembering. And in this cold . . .

It is strange how things happen sometimes. Don't you think? Who would have thought that Patón would end up as he did, driving a trailer truck up north, after who he was around here? When we saw each other for the last time, in Tancay, Patón already had a feeling that something was going to change in his life. When you asked him about the incident with the woman and her son, he did not want to say anything. Don't you remember? Maybe he was preparing himself. Maybe he had a feeling that very soon there would be much more that he would not be able to talk about, that the police would chase him, for no good reason, until they made him disappear from these shores. It seems that life itself prepares us to deal with whatever lies ahead, Alejandro. . . . I am going to tell you again what happened.

The incident happened in the mid-1970s, during a very hot summer. It was probably for that very reason that the woman and her son had gone to the beach. They must have wanted to feel the ocean breeze. For some reason, the summer camp was closed. In those days they used to close it on a whim. The poor watchman would spend days just watching buzzards. But anyway . . . I remember that the woman wore a yellow dress, black shoes with high heels, imagine that, and a white Panama hat. She must have been about thirty. Humming, she walked, floated rather, along the rocks, the paths, the edge of the precipice. She was rather attractive. She would hold on to her hat with one hand, against the high wind.

The son must have been about eight. He was well dressed: leather shoes, blue pants, white shirt with black buttons. But he was a mischievous boy. He was into everything. He had to be told not to step on the fishing lines. He teased the water. Spitting. Throwing rocks into it. Running when the waves would come. The fishermen told him to stop doing that and to go back to his mother, but he would not listen. He cursed the ocean. He spat into the wind.

It must have been about four in the afternoon. The wind from El Dorado was picking up, and the tide was coming in. The woman had sat down on La Mesa, to watch a school of dolphins passing by. Lalo and I were on La Punta, catching chita. The men on La Pared were already leaving. . . . Then we heard, as if in a tunnel, the scream from the woman. We turned around to see her. She was running toward the water; the wind was taking her hat. "My son! My son!" she screamed.

We ran to see what had happened, but the boy was not there anymore. There was nothing. Just then, as we stood there not knowing what to do, boom! We heard a huge wave and saw the boy in the air. Way up. The foam around him was ashen. I saw his eyes. It seemed that he already knew he was going to die. He stretched out his little arms. He coughed. The mother could only wail from the rocks. She was crying so much, they say, that her weeping could be heard all the way to Besique. Worse yet—perhaps tasting fear, the sea became ever more violent. And to add to the misfortune, the poor woman ended up slipping. She tumbled down and was tossed around in the foam. Once there, she now forgot how to swim, if she ever knew. She only punched at the waves.

All of us stood like dazed cochos . . . paralyzed. . . . Maybe everything was meant to happen the way it did because it all happened so suddenly. . . . I saw everything from far away, blinded by the setting sun, as if in a dream. There were four chiteros on La Mesa. They did not do anything. Imagine that. Nobody tried to save them. It should not be like that. A Good Fisherman tries, however he can. Maybe that is why the fishermen did not want to talk about the incident for such a long time. . . . But Patón, yes. He jumped in.

In those days Patón came to fish once in a while. He was a good friend. We used to call him Patón because he had feet as big as boats. But, in fact, the people of Villa María gave him the nickname because he was a really good soccer player. He was known for his grit. He was a professional. People would come from Lima, from Trujillo, even from Arequipa looking for him to play on their teams. But Patón was always attached to his home turf. He would go away for a month or two, but he would always come back. Until the problems with terrorism came, that is . . . then he really went away for good.

He must have been sitting behind the rocks because I did not see him until he appeared running, taking off his shoes, his shirt, his pants. And he dove head first into the foam. He swam up to the woman who was still punching the waves. "A line! Roseteros!" he shouted to us. Only then did we react. What a shameful thing, damn it. . . . He tried to help her. He tried to talk to her. But she could no longer hear. The waves were hitting her on the head. The boy had already disappeared.

I threw her my roseta. I aimed and placed it on her dress, right near the waistband. But by now the woman did not want to be saved. The sea had entered her head and her soul. She was punching Patón. She was scratching him all over. Poor Patón, he was bleeding. Then it got even worse. Once the sea had tasted human blood, it began to crash all over the place. It almost reached way up to the paths. Patón tried one more time. He dove underwater and lifted the woman from below, but she broke free and disappeared again. I pulled as hard as I could . . . I felt I was losing her. The line was humming in the air. But there was nothing to be done, it broke, even though it was Payaso. It broke. Patón got out as best he could, all scratched up.

Three days later we found the woman's body washed ashore near Las Dos Hermanas. She had no eyes. They had been eaten by octopuses. We never found the boy's body. Patón did not go to

Tancay for almost a year. We would meet him in Chimbote: "Let's go fishing, Patón!" "No, I have a lot to do," he would answer.

Only later did he return to the rocks. He was with us for a long time. He became a Good Fisherman. But you should know that even a Good Fisherman at times can lose his serenity: in the early '80s, Patón got involved in defending newspaper boys. He said that the boys were being exploited by the businessmen, that they did not even have a place to sleep, that they needed social security. The police accused him of being a terrorist, as it happened with you, and they chased him all the way to Tumbes. He lives up there now, with his family. Genaro says that he drives a white trailer truck as far as Quito, where Atahualpa came from. Who knows. Maybe life will give him another push, and we will see him around here once again. A lot of people in Villa María think he will come back one of these days. If he comes, I will tell him that you asked about him.

10
Hermelindo

So then, Alejandro, many foolish people have died on the rocks of Tancay. If one sets foot there with an unclean heart, that world pulls him in. I had the bad luck of knowing some of them. Hermelindo, for example, the one who drowned at Las Dos Hermanas. . . . Maybe it is time I told you his story. Do not worry too much about me. Of course, it is a little painful to remember what happened, but we also have to see it as a kind of return, because I was still young then. I was catching chita everywhere: El Dorado, El Patillo Ahogado, the pier at Besique, Las Dos Hermanas. . . . There were a lot of fish. The waters were clean. The sun felt nice and hot upon us. The nights were like this one: full of stars. And my body did not hurt without reason. . . . Although Genaro says that every old fisherman carries waves splashing around inside him. That can't be. . . .

The story begins the day that I went fishing and met a pair of twins who had just arrived from the highlands. One of them, Paulo, was chubby and dark-skinned. The other, Hermelindo, was thin and gringo. They had come from Cajamarca, where they say there are many blue-eyed people and many twins. They smelled of eucalyptus, Alejandro; because they also say that Cajamarca is full of eucalyptus trees. . . . In any case, they asked me to teach them to fish. I had never taught before. But remembering don Tico, my own teacher, I agreed to teach them what I could. From the beginning, the teaching seemed easy because the twins were very intelligent. They learned very quickly how to read the foam, the whirlpools, the color of the sky. Things were going so well that in a few days we were going everywhere together, happy as could be. Until on a bad day in winter we decided to fish at Las Dos Hermanas.

Everything started out fine. The sky was clear. The tide low. We brought good ropes, water, and plenty of bait. We crossed over to the second sister carefully. As one should. And so, well, we sat down to fish. There were a lot of fish. We would throw the line out and bam! a big chita. After a short time we decided, as we should have, that it was time to leave. The tide was still low. . . . We jumped to the first sister and swam to the beach. Our sacks were full. It was time to go home and rest.

But then strange things began to happen. After going a few steps on the beach, Hermelindo said that he wanted to go back to Las Dos Hermanas. "They don't bite like this every day," he said with a strange gleam in his eyes. Paulo looked at me hesitantly, not knowing how to answer his brother. I told them that it was already time to leave. "We have all that we can carry," I told them. But Hermelindo insisted on going back. It was only then that I realized that I had not taught them control. He even became insolent and told me I did not have to stay if I did not want to. "The tide is coming in," I told him. But the blue-eyed twin was very obstinate. He turned around and started walking back. With all that fish! Imagine that, Alejandro. I saw in Paulo's face a plea that I should stay. It was insane. Why be so greedy? To this day I do not know why I stayed. Maybe everything happened as it was meant to. Maybe the destiny of human beings is already written in the stars, as they say. . . .

And so we returned. We jumped to the second sister with all the fish on our shoulders. We knew that the next low tide would not come until late at night. We knew that now we would just have to sit there and wait. We would need to have a lot of patience. The fish would stay fresh in the cold. . . . They were not biting very much now. But nevertheless we had so much fish that we were throwing back even the medium-size ones. Foolishness overtook us, Alejandro. . . . Then, all at once, Hermelindo was seized by the idea of wanting to leave: "We have to cross before it gets darker," he said. "Before los nocturnos see us. If not, they will come and take everything, and tomorrow there will be nothing left."

I do not know why we sometimes do things knowing that they

are going to turn out badly. But that is how we humans are. If it were not so, maybe there would not even be evil in the world. . . . We tied ourselves to one another with the ropes. And I tell you that at that very moment, like a well-deserved curse, a thick cloud came to stand still in the sky; everything turned very dark. On top of that, the tide started coming in very strong. The water splashed all around, seeking to cover everything. Now, of course, we had to jump long and deftly to the first sister. . . . We should have left all the fish on the second sister. Better yet, we should have returned it all to the sea.

I crossed first. Once I reached the other side, I stretched out my hand to help Hermelindo. But the gringo had too much fish. He did not make it. He fell like a rock between Las Dos Hermanas. Splash! And even as the water was sucking him down, the fool would not let go of the sack. "Drop the sack, damn it! Drop it!" Paulo yelled to him. Hermelindo did not hear him. In the blink of an eye the sea sucked him in.

The ropes were strong. From a fishing boat. We pulled with all our might, but just then my rope broke against the barnacles and the submerged rocks. Hermelindo spun around and was lost in the night. Paulo still had him on his rope. He was crying. "Drop it! Drop it!" But Hermelindo could not hear anymore. The sea had entered his soul. And then Paulo could no longer hold onto the rope. It must have been slimy. It slipped through his fingers like a snake. We could no longer see Hermelindo. The sea became violent. Its waves were breaking over the top of the second sister as Paulo kept calling his brother by name: "Hermelindo! Hermelindo!" The poor man was going crazy. He ran up and down on the second sister, with the water licking his heels, looking for his brother in that darkness. And there I was, not knowing what to do. I did not even dare to go back to the second sister to console him. The sea had won.

It was a cold night, with dense shadows. We had nothing to eat. But how could I leave Paulo alone on the other side? And so I sat down against a high crag and waited for someone to come. But nobody came. Not even los nocturnos. Nobody. I had to spend the night there, listening to Paulo calling to his brother . . . until morning came, and I was happy to hear the voices of two cordeleros.

I signaled to them like crazy, and fortunately they saw me. They approached. On their way they found Hermelindo's fish strewn on the beach. I had to shout to tell them what had happened.

The cordeleros swam to the first sister, and from there they saw Paulo on the second. The poor man was just sitting, rubbing his hands together. They asked him to tie himself to the ropes, to jump to the first sister. But fear had welled up in Paulo's soul. He could not hear. He was gone. After trying for a long time, I had to jump to the second sister, tie him with three ropes, and help to pull him over the turning tide. Fortunately, the sea let him go. But it had gotten inside of him. It would not let him stop trembling.

By then there were many people on the beach. They came to try to do something. But their pleas were useless. At first, Paulo sat down on the beach to cry and to look at his hands. He rubbed them; he shook them. . . . Later, Paulo got up from the sand looking at the sea like a madman and began to run along the beach. He went up and down, calling to his brother. He did not want to stop. We had to take him to the hospital in Chimbote. They say that from there he went up to Cajamarca. He never again came back to Tancay while he was alive. . . .

I learned then that to be a Good Fisherman it is not enough to be intelligent. One has to learn other things. One has to learn calmness, control. The sea is like a mother; she feeds us all. But without calmness, without control, we cross the line. Then she abandons us, she punishes us. That is what is happening now with the damn factories. They are offending the sea. One of these days we are all going to have to pay the price for what people like Canchero are doing.

Carmela

It is not only humans who can have a clean heart, Alejandro. Animals can, too, only in their own way. There is enough serenity, patience, for everyone. Hawks, dolphins, turtles—all have their own patience. They measure things. They do not hurry. They see the world with old eyes. Sometimes a human with a clean heart becomes attached to an animal. Sometimes an animal with a clean heart becomes attached to a human. That is what happened with Carmela. It was a very special case. . . .

When Besique was still a port, there was a man in Villa María who drank a lot, mistreated his wife, cursed at his neighbors, and kicked his dog. Carmela, the dog, was huge and had sleepy eyes. She was as big as an ox. But so skinny! You could count her ribs from a distance.

No one knew how it was that the man came to own Carmela. Some used to say that he had stolen her from a Russian circus that had come to the barriada. Others used to say that the man had brought her from the border with Ecuador, from a breeding farm where they cross dogs with alpacas. But, for his part, the man never said anything. He let people invent stories. The truth was that nobody else in Chimbote had a dog like Carmela.

At first, even though the man did not feed her well, he was proud of her. He would walk all around the barriada with the dog by his side. He would often get drunk and pass out on the street. Carmela would lie down by his side to look after him. There she would wait for him, patiently. She was a good dog.

In time, as happens with dogs from a barriada, Carmela got

pregnant. So she went to hide behind some boxes in the man's house. There she gave birth to six puppies. Barriada puppies, with nameless fathers. . . . But because of it, a foolish neighbor claimed one of the puppies for himself. "That one has the face of my Guardián," he said, pointing to a black puppy with white spots.

Things went well between the man and the neighbor for some time. They even spent the night at La Cabra's place, which at that time had just opened. But one day, as always happens between drunkards, they ended up fighting. In a moment of blind anger, the neighbor reached into Carmela's lair with the intention of taking her puppy. Of course, being a good mother, Carmela bit his hand.

Then came the brawl. Dogs and men knocked each other down for hours until the police came with their rifles and took the two men to the station. The man could not get back to Villa María for three days. And when he came back, he was more bitter than ever. He was not the same with his dog. He blamed her for his being thrown in jail. He would kick her whenever he wanted. He would not feed her. Sometimes his wife, a very small and frail woman, would try to stop him. The man would then hit his wife and his dog. That is how it all began. . . . As doña Pelagia says, though, sooner or later everything seeks its level; even evil and hatred can last only so long. Even now, even these misfortunes that are putting wrinkles on our faces and draining our spirits will pass, Alejandro. They will pass. . . .

A few weeks later Carmela got sick. She had big sores all over her body. They hurt her so much that the poor thing would spend the nights howling. She hardly ate at all, and she would sleep standing up. Her ears withered. The drainage from her eyes covered her face . . . until the man could not stand her anymore. He told half the world that the dog stunk and that he wanted to sell her. Perhaps it was in those days that people started calling him "Dog Killer."

It must have been in those days, too, that the man decided to get rid of Carmela. She had become a stingray's spine lodged in his unclean heart. He tried to do it in several ways. One time he took her in a colectivo all the way to Santa. He told Carmela to sit and wait for him, then he came home secretly. On the way to his house the man met some of his friends. Feeling happy, he had a few drinks.

But when he finally arrived home, he found Carmela there, wagging her tail with joy. The man almost went mad. He yelled curses at her. But because he was very drunk, he just went to sleep.

A few weeks later he tried again. This time he put Carmela on a trailer bound for Lima. Since he knew where the trailer trucks stopped, he waited till nightfall and brought the dog on a rope. When he saw that one truck was leaving, he threw Carmela onto the trailer's platform and tied her to the railing. That night he went to sleep contented, thinking that at last he had gotten rid of her.

The next day the man awoke happy. He walked around like a peacock. On the following day he was so happy he invited his friends to eat and to drink. But, as you probably have already guessed, on the third day a trailer truck stopped in front of his house. The driver told him that in Lima he had run into a friend who was on his way to Arequipa hauling metal. The friend had told him that in Chimbote someone had tied an enormous dog onto his trailer. The friend, who knew the owner, asked him to return her because the animal was very sad. "Since it was on my way," said the driver, "I brought her." So there was Carmela once again, wagging her tail, jumping for joy.

The man tried to get rid of the dog in other ways. Once he gave her rat poison, but a gringa from the Peace Corps saved her with some sort of laxative. Carmela spent the whole day relieving herself until she had nothing left, all over the man's house. . . . On another occasion the man tried to sell her to an Italian circus, as food for the lions. But the owner of the circus would not take her. He said that the dog was too skinny, and he was afraid she would make his animals sick.

Meanwhile, the neighbors realized what the man was trying to do. They began to turn their backs on him. Nobody wanted to eat or drink with him now. The children called him "Dog Killer" from behind their mothers' skirts. Days. Weeks. Until the man could not stand it anymore. On a very hot Saturday in March, he decided to get rid of Carmela once and for all.

He got up early, put some hooks and lines in a bag, and left with Carmela for the beach, with the story that he was going fishing.

They walked together along Veintisiete de Octubre, they crossed La Playa Desierta, they passed by Tancay, Las Dos Hermanas, La Cocina . . . until they arrived at the pier in Besique.

They must have arrived at about midday. Poor Carmela's tongue was hanging out from so much walking. . . . The sun was fixed in the center of the sky. There were a lot of people swimming at the beach. The radios and record players were outdoing each other. . . . And so the man took his dog over the loose boards of the pier all the way to the very end. He walked, serious and looking straight ahead, and Carmela followed him with adoring eyes and her tongue hanging out.

When they arrived at the end of the pier, the man bent down to the dog, as if to pet her. He put his arms around her skinny body and lifted her up, tight against himself, as if they were a pair of dancers. The man then spun around and around with the dog in his arms. People must have thought he had gone mad. And the sun stayed fixed in the center of the sky. Just then, all of a sudden, becoming as flexible as a whip, the man tried to hurl Carmela into the ocean. Feeling herself in danger, Carmela was scared. Who wouldn't be? That is why, at the last moment, the dog embraced her owner with all her might. The man had not expected that, so he lost his balance. They fell into the water, like two lovers. . . .

After a moment of sheer rage, when the man ran out of insults, he realized that he did not know how to swim. He then tried to grab onto the pier's black and greasy posts. But, as if on purpose, the sea began to push him farther and farther out. That is when fear entered his soul. The man began to cry, to splash around. From far away, the people realized that he was drowning. This was how all his wickedness was going to end. . . .

But no. Only God knows why, Carmela swam to him, turned to one side and offered him her tail. The man grabbed the tail in desperation, and Carmela began to pull for the beach. She seemed really tired. Her tongue was floating on the water. The sun was so strong above, but she kept going. We were all watching her, quivering in the waves of light over the ocean. Inspired by her clean heart, perhaps, we cheered her on: "Come on, Carmela! Come on!" . . . And yes, after a long struggle, Carmela brought her owner to the beach. When the man stepped on the sand, he was still crying. He could not stop. He embraced Carmela. She licked his face.

Later, when the man had calmed down, he returned to Villa María. We saw him pass by La Cocina, Las Dos Hermanas, Tancay, La Playa Desierta . . . with Carmela by his side. . . . From then on he was a changed man. He never again hit either his wife or his dog. And they say that when the earthquake came, the man risked his life to save several people.

If only things would always turn out that way, right, Alejandro? Then, yes, one would not have to wring his hands thinking, remembering. . . .

12
The King of the Mojarrilla

It would be nice to remember in full detail all that we did, all that we felt. Don't you think so, Alejandro? But it is not possible. We must content ourselves with fragments instead. It is all we can do. . . . And besides, look at that star that is blinking so bright. They say it is possible that it no longer exists, that its light no longer has a source, that its source has been spent. The same with our stories, Alejandro. Because the truth is that of Tancay very little is left. . . . Our fragments will I hope be sufficient tonight so that you can find your sitio. . . . But to continue remembering, it must be said that, in spite of the mist that licks our memory, the image of El Rey still persists. . . .

No one remembers his name anymore, but he had walked along those beaches since before I arrived here. His image is very cloudy now, as if he had melded into our memory. They say he was an old, thin man, with a little black goatee and a frayed straw hat. They say he had long arms and fingers, like an octopus. They say he was a descendant of the Chan Chan. And they also say that he was from the highlands. From Cajamarca. Who knows. With so many stories, our memory plays tricks on us. . . . He came to know you, Alejandro, although you probably no longer remember. "The boy goes around with knots in his soul," he told me when you left. . . .

He had married a woman who always walked around dressed in mourning. He had a young son, two younger daughters, a yellowish dog, a chestnut donkey, and a milking cow. He lived on the edge of the desert, behind some dunes that had stopped walking near where Villa María was later founded. I used to see him walking along Veintisiete de Octubre, pulling his donkey and pushing his cow. He would tie his animals by the marshes and go to the pier at Besique to catch mojarrilla.

They say that El Rey caught so many mojarrillas one time that there was no place to walk on the pier. The croaking of the fish was so loud it could be heard all the way to Tancay. That day, El Rey had to take his mojarrillas by train. It took eight stevedores all afternoon to load them. What do you think of that? And that was not all. They say that El Rey had forgotten his bait that day. He caught them all with the shoestrings from the old shoes he wore!

They say El Rey's son wanted to be a radio announcer and that he practiced by announcing the fishing derby in Tancay. He would sit on a high crag and go on for hours celebrating the luck of the fishermen: "Here comes the chita on the right, the *viña* appears at the left, now the pampanito takes the lead, the tramboyo is passing them all. . . . " El Rey was a man of immense patience. He was so patient that he would let flies make love on his eyelashes. But the boy was so annoying that even El Rey could not stand it.

He told him to be quiet, several times. It was not because he wanted silence to fish. El Rey could catch mojarrilla dancing or sleeping. It was for the rest of the fishermen that he wanted silence—for those who were fishing for chita, and all for whom the sound of the human voice was something sacred.

The boy would not stop. El Rey pleaded and pleaded, but the boy would not stop. Then El Rey got up from his sitio and began to announce his own derby: "Here comes the chita on the left. Aha! The viña at the right. And now a huge beast comes up the middle. He is coming for the brat who is making so much noise!" They say that the boy took off running to save himself. But El Rey followed him at a mule's pace all the way to Chimbote, found him, put a fresh mojarrilla in his mouth, and brought him back to his high crag at Tancay. They say that the boy kept the mojarrilla in his mouth for the rest of the day. Lucky that it was already late! The thing is that he never announced the derby again.

But I should tell you that this story might not be true. Those derby announcement were the baby steps of the one who was to become Viroca, the famous rock-and-roll star of the valley. But let us

leave that story for later. . . . I don't know, Alejandro, but the night is lending itself to remembering, in spite of the cold and the pain in my body. It must be that, in spite of everything, there is something sweet about returning to the past. It must be that we feel somewhat at ease, even when reliving moments of anger and sadness, because all those roads are already familiar to us. . . .

In any case, they say El Rey plugged the sewer pipes of the damn factories with seaweed when they began to drain the sludge into the ocean. The waste got backed up, and the rats of the port came out to invade streets, houses, everything. Not even the mansions at the naval base were safe. The admirals and their wives had to sleep with sentinels for fear of being eaten alive. That lasted for days. But, in the end, after a great ordeal the engineers unplugged the pipes. Canchero posted permanent guards where the sludge was draining.

They say that El Rey could speak with all the animals. That this is why he spoke with the last cocho, a brown pelican with white stripes who lived around here, to find out why all the other cochos had left these shores and where the tramboyos, the *borrachos*, the *lenguados*, all those fish who had disappeared overnight, were now swimming. He spent hours talking with the dying cocho, they say. When night came, he took him to his house and fed him corn and mojarrilla. The cocho lived there for several weeks.

But, as we know, all living things have their own way of being, their own sitio, and the sitio of the cocho is the sea. This cocho could not go on living in the midst of cows and chickens. He missed the salt water. So one day he told El Rey that he wanted to die in his own sitio. That is why El Rey brought him back to Tancay. I saw him, far away, walking north with the cocho under his arm. But others say that the cocho came sitting on the donkey. And Genaro told me the other day that the cocho was already dead when El Rey put him in the water. I think that as soon as he felt the water, the cocho let himself be carried by the current. . . . The thing is that El Rey stopped talking for weeks. His eyes were looking inward.

Perhaps it was in those days that El Rey decided that it was his time to disappear as well. Maybe he wanted to go like the cocho. Looking for his sitio, perhaps. The thing is that he sold his milking cow and his little donkey, told everyone to leave the rocks, dressed in mourning like his wife, and disappeared. Some say that he died some years back, one day when the waters of Tancay turned red at daybreak. Because, as you know, when someone very special dies, the waters give the sign. Others say that El Rey was killed by Canchero and the admirals who never forgave him for the nights of horror they had spent.

As for me, I think that El Rey became a *gentil*. That is why people say so many different things about him. Because they are all true. Because truths are worth something only when somebody believes them. El Rey has melded into our memory, to mix with our sins, with our dreams, with our truths. He must now be walking over there in the desert, as patient and playful as ever. Not for nothing he gave himself the nickname El Rey de la Mojarrilla.

i3
Cacho, the Crabber

How beautiful it would be if we could distill life into words, Alejandro. Maybe then everything would have been different. Maybe you would have listened to us and not have suffered this disgrace. But only life teaches us how to live. This is why the Good Fisherman never uses words in place of experience. If he has advice to give, he gives it obliquely, so that it will not preclude anything.

In truth, it is as if the good advice were already known and we only have to remember it. There are new lessons only once in a while, when the world has changed enough. But we should not feel too smug and fail to listen to those who have lived long because, like time, experience is accumulated. And all that we accumulate shows up in what we are doing, thinking, eating, living. Good advice, like truths, is of no value outside of life, and a life that does not embrace good advice is not worth much. . . .

El Rey also gave advice, though not always obliquely; sometimes he would give advice when the listener's ears were quite open. That is what happened with Cacho, the crabber. We have to remember him, too. What do you say, Alejandro? And his story begins when you had just arrived in Tancay, before they built the summer camp. What can I tell you? . . . Cacho was a young crabber who wanted to be a fisherman. But he was impatient. He wanted to do everything right away. He did not want anyone to help him.

One day Cacho caught three sacks of crabs this big. He sold them quickly at the markets in Chimbote, and he bought himself a hook, a line, and a sinker. The next day he was in Tancay at daybreak in order to meet up and walk with the chiteros. He made them miserable with his annoying questions. He told them stories and walked along carrying himself as if he were an old fisherman. He was a foolish boy.

When the chiteros arrived at Tancay, they spread out. Cacho followed them with long strides and set up to fish from a high rock, looking all around google-eyed. And he had good luck. He was the first to catch chita. He was so happy that he stood up from his spot holding the fish up in the air for everyone to see. When he got another bite, he was even more full of himself. If at first he had cast short, now he was casting long, using more and more line.

When he had finally let out all of his line, he realized that he needed to secure the cork spool. He could have done it like the tourists do, like you yourself used to do, with a small stone. But no, the great fisherman put the cork in his pocket. It was a small cork, like the ones you find at La Playa Desierta. . . . In any case, the fool must have had the cork in his pocket for about an hour. He was catching good chitas until, suddenly, he felt a really strong pull. "Wow!" he thought, "This is a really big chita!" And he began to reel in the line, feeling an enormous weight, a straight and steady pull. His whole body was filled with joy.

When the line was straight down against the rocks, Cacho could finally see what he had hooked: a turtle the size of a cow! He pointed to it and burst out laughing, who knows whether from glee or from embarrassment. . . . At any rate, now it was time for him to find a way to let it go. But, no. Maybe it was from the anger of feeling ridiculed or from the foolishness of wanting to do what nobody till then had ever done, Cacho decided to bring in that turtle. Imagine that! When the chiteros saw what he was trying to do, they yelled to him to let the turtle go. But with his heart surely unclean by now, Cacho wanted to land it however he could. The turtle, for his part, followed Cacho's tomfoolery for quite a while. As I have been telling you, even turtles can be patient. But only up to a certain point. Because when the turtle decided that he had already been detoured too far off his course, he began to pull like a turtle. With his heart even more unclean, Cacho held onto the line with all his might. The turtle remained a prisoner.

But then the turtle lifted his head out of the water, turned around, and looked toward the rocks. "What does this fool want?" he must have said. . . . Meanwhile, the chiteros kept yelling at Cacho to let it go. They saw him, like a madman, leaning over backwards for pulling so hard. . . . But, in fact, the whole thing had changed: by then Cacho no longer wanted to land the turtle. For some reason, a premonition perhaps, he had let go of his anger. Now all he wanted was to retrieve his line that was whistling in the wind. . . . But by then the turtle had already made his own decision: he put his head under water and began to paddle. Slap, slap, slap. Like that. Cacho had no choice but to give him more and more line . . . until he had no more line to give. Since the turtle did not stop paddling, Cacho feared that the turtle was going to take it all. . . . That was when, resigned, even though still feigning reluctance, the fool tried to take the cork out of his pocket . . . but now it was too late. . . . The turtle had taken him from his spot and was pulling him like an old rag from rock to rock. Cacho tried to stand firm here, there, but he was out of control, with his pants stretched out in front of him.

Feeling like the turtle's prisoner, the boy got really scared and began to cry. He wanted to take off his pants, but he could not take off even his belt. Maybe the turtle sensed his fear. Maybe the turtle was angry. Who knows. But he kept on going, heading out to sea. The boy's feet and hands were cut and bleeding from so many jumps and stops. Seeing him like that, the chiteros ran to help him, but they knew that it was in vain because they were all too far away. It seemed that Cacho was going to drown.

Then, when it seemed all was lost, they heard the voice of El Rey, who was passing by La Punta with his sack of mojarrillas: "Bite the line! Bite the line, damn it!" The boy, despite all his pain and his fear, recognized the voice of El Rey. Because they say that El Rey could speak so strongly he could shorten all distances and soar over time itself.

Desperate, with his last bit of strength, Cacho bent over and bit the line. As if by a miracle, the line broke. We all breathed a sigh of relief, our spirits began returning to our bodies. . . . But the boy was not saved yet. He had lost his balance and could not stop himself from falling head over heels between the rocks and the foam. The waves, as always when they smell death, took advantage and began to break even higher. They hit him on the head, on the back. They disoriented him. They tossed him around like an old cork in a whirlpool. Yes, Alejandro, Cacho was drowning.

At that moment, El Rey dropped his sack, went down into the choppy waters, stood firmly on the barnacles, stretched out his enormous right hand with its enormous fingers and fished the boy out by the hair. He lifted him up like a wet rag and carried him hanging in the air until he dropped him on the beach. As soon as Cacho set foot on the sand, El Rey shook him by the shoulders and slapped him in the face three times. The chiteros at La Cocina heard the blows and thought they were the thunderclaps of summer.

When Cacho regained his senses, El Rey looked him straight in the eye and yelled at him with a voice like a seal, telling him that he had to begin at the beginning: "That is," he told him, "if you are interested in becoming a Good Fisherman . . . "

That is how the boy resigned himself to cultivate patience, to know the play of the foam, to clean his heart. That is why, even now, when Cacho remembers El Rey, he feels only gratitude.

That is also why I prolonged my time as a teacher. I taught the boy what I had learned from don Tico. Not with words or with books, as you used to argue education should be. But with the hands. With the eyes. With the heart. Things had to be done from the beginning: "This is how to tie on the hook; now you do it. This is how to look at the foam; now tell me what it says." In that way I, too, became a student. Because experiences and truths left tucked away end up dying, Alejandro. They must be lived. And to teach the things that one knows is like living them again.

14
The Humble Fisherman

It is not that I am a great teacher. There are many things I do not know, Alejandro. Rather, I am humble, like my ancestors. Because I was born in San Jacinto, over there where there used to be cornfields and now everything is just sugar cane. Not like you who were raised in El Miraflores, as you said, wearing shoes and short pants. We used to have a little adobe house at the very edge of the desert. But we did not work at a hacienda. We had a little ranch, with flowers and everything. But then came years of drought. Even the cactuses dried up. So we had to sell the little plot of land in order to try our luck around here. This must have been around the time when they began to build the steel mill.

We all came: my mother, who was with us until just three years ago; my aunt Hortensia, who was touched in the head and died buried in the earthquake of '70; my Aurora, who must be outside with doña Pelagia, consoling your friends as God commands; my two oldest sons; seven nieces and nephews; and a brother-in-law who had just been discharged from the army and did not want to stay behind to clean irrigation ditches for others. We came because, as I was telling you, in those days the port was overflowing with hope. But all that glitters is not gold. . . .

We could not find work. The youngsters missed the land, the river that came down from the highlands, wild at times, but mostly tame and crystalline. We quickly went through the money we had brought. We were desperate, and desperation is relentless; it dances in the soul like the foam around the rocks of Tancay. But, thank God, one day we met doña Pelagia in the market. She must have

57

seen me like a lost cocho and had pity on me. As if she had known me from before, she advised me to go and find a way to make a living around El Dorado. It was because of her that I became a fisherman. I started out collecting seaweed, snails, mussels, hairy crabs. That is how we learned to eat *ceviche*. . . .

A little later I met don Tico. The blessed man was so old that you could not even see his eyes for all the wrinkles he had. It seemed that he had been fishing from those rocks since the beginning of the world. Sometimes I think that he was one of Los Gentiles doing me a favor. He knew everything about fishing: how to read the shadows, how to feel the fish, how to see the colors of the moon, how to understand the dance of the foam. But, most of all, he knew how to be patient and to keep his heart clean. Because in order to become a Good Fisherman, as with becoming anything that is worthwhile, one has to have a clean heart.

I learned to catch all kinds of fish at El Dorado, but I could not stay there for very long. The sludge from the damn factories soon covered everything. The sea became like soup. The snails came out to die on the sand. The crabs lost their hair. The lenguados spun around on the surface of the water until they died. The octopuses lost their legs. Years later, as if the world had high and low tides like the ocean, the sludge retreated a little, and the fish returned. But then very few and not of all kinds. In any case, that was when don Tico began to let go of life.

He would walk in those hills for hours without talking. He would stutter. He would stare as if he had been touched in the head by a ghost. He would eat only dried seaweed. . . . I used to follow him everywhere, a little scared, trying to help him in any way I could. For weeks . . . until one day he told me he wanted to die. He gave me his fishing bundle, including two black cork spools, and he laid down to rest in the sand. He told me not to wake him up anymore. . . . I buried him near El Cerro Colorado. Genaro says that when don Tico let go of life, the sea was bright red at dawn, and thousands of white herons descended on the entire Santa Valley. In those days Lalo was born.

15
Lalo

Do you notice how the smell of boiled fish does not show up anywhere around here? Strange, isn't it? It seems that doña Pelagia was right: memories come forth more easily in this backyard. It seems that even time goes slower or faster to help us. In this bluish light even my wrinkles look different. My bones do not complain as much anymore. . . . More than anything, I feel your sentiments deep inside me, Alejandro. And the truth is that I really appreciate your gratitude. . . . But we must go on remembering still. . . .

When Lalo was growing up, the world of Tancay had changed; there were already too many fisherman and very few chita. The sludge had not yet made the turn around El Dorado, but the signs were everywhere. The cochos were abandoning the valley, the penguins no longer came to bask in the sun. That is why I sent the older children to the school in Villa María. . . . I know you are going to say that I always believed your story that education is more important than anything. But no, Alejandro, . . . the truth is that I came to accept only that the children had to know the world of the city, that they had to learn to defend themselves in the world that was given to them. Fortunately, Floro became a merchant, and Julián went into teaching.

As for Lalo, he was born different. He dreamed of the sea. He lived to hear the sea birds and the waves. He had respect for the water, but not fear. It seems that our traditions, the past, were more alive in his blood. And so, when he finished primary school, we resigned ourselves to the fact that he would be a rock fisherman. And if he were going to be a fisherman, then he would have to learn to be a good one. I wanted Genaro to teach him, but in those days he was still enthralled with los nocturnos. He did not stop living that upside-down life until Canchero was killed, when it was already too late for anything. . . .

Lalo had to start from the beginning. First I took him to La Playa Desierta. He had to learn how to find the fishing spots, to unwind the line in a high wind, to throw it strong against the tide, to feel the fish in the distance. . . . But those really were not the main things. They were merely necessary gestures. The important thing was that he learn to have patience, that he begin to learn how to clean his heart. That is why he had to stay at La Playa Desierta for days at a time. Alone. Without catching anything. With the sun and the wind. Fish biting or not biting. Because patience is not always rewarded. If one expects rewards, one has not learned anything.

After that I took him to El Dorado. On three different trips. On the first trip I asked him to catch *pejeblanco*, the goldeneye tilefish. He had to learn to respect the fish's sharp mind. Because the pejeblanco makes pirouettes in the air. He knows a thousand ways to escape. He anticipates your movements. You think he is already yours, when bam! he's gone. By making fun of him, the pejeblanco taught Lalo to quiet his heart, to let time pass, like the wind. He is a good teacher, the pejeblanco.

I am sure that on that first trip Lalo must have wanted to give it all up. He must have felt completely alone, abandoned, among those mute crags, looking at the sea. He must have felt like I did when don Tico took me there for the first time: like an intruder, as if a million eyes were watching me from the shadows, from the streams of water falling back to the sea, from the thick foam, from everywhere. . . . The pejeblanco must have eaten well that day. . . . That trip lasted several days. I cannot even remember now. . . .

On the second trip I took him to Cerro Colorado. A high mountain. You walked along the base of it, Alejandro, but with different intentions. You went there like nothing more than a tourist. You saw only red rocks, I imagine. You did not see the *pitajaya* cactuses in bloom, the fine sand resting against the rocks, announcing hot or cool weather. You were always looking far away, searching for justice, as you used to say, in your head. You walked blindly among the foothills. . . . In any case. From those heights I pointed out to him La Playa de los Chungos. You can see it so clearly. It seems like the sun lies down to rest in that solitude. I asked him to look for the fishing spot surrounded by seven gray crags and told him that I would be waiting for him on the top of Cerro Colorado.

I took him there because the Good Fisherman is not rowdy or nosy. The Good Fisherman is serene, humble. Those gray crags teach humility; they teach communion with what surrounds us. When I was learning, they filled me with strange emotions. The silence is so strong there that one feels very small. Empty. Wanting to cry. There is no one there to console you. Only absence. But, of course, I knew that don Tico would help him, that he would always watch over Lalo. . . . Lalo stayed there for several days.

On the third trip I took him down to La Playa de los Chungos itself, from where you can truly enjoy the sun setting on the ocean. Lalo had to spend the night there. Alone. He could not fish, eat, sleep, or move from the sitio. Because the Good Fisherman becomes one with the night, with his dark side. The Good Fisherman embraces his deepest fears and makes them his own. This is how he completes himself; he recognizes himself. After that, fishing becomes something secondary. In truth, the Good Fisherman fishes because he wants to. Like Genaro. He could do anything else. Even become a dancer. You must have seen him with his greasy pants, with his crooked smile, and you probably had pity on him. That is how he is. Cunning. He does not care if anyone understands him. He is a whole bundle of questions.

Lalo stayed there for several days. He lived on pitajaya cactus and seaweed until, on a morning of his own choosing, he left La Playa de los Chungos. Only then did he realize that I had not been waiting for him, like a silent huaco, on Cerro Colorado. He then realized that the Good Fisherman feels, finds, makes fellowship, even if his friends are far away. Silence, fear, even Las Almitas are good company. You have only to grasp the meaning of their nature, of their way of being. That is how it is. Don't you think so, Alejandro?

After our trips to El Dorado, which I think lasted a long time, about three months, Lalo went alone to El Patillo Ahogado. It is too bad that he is not around to tell us about it, no? His leaving for the north is kind of sad. And if he does not find a place to fish? If you had been around here, in spite of all your indolence, maybe he would not have gone. . . . But, anyway, he knows what he is doing. Besides, Genaro tells me that they talk now and then. But let us not lose the thread of our remembrance. . . . In El Patillo Ahogado Lalo had to learn only one thing: to get the tramboyo out of its hole.

Once the tramboyo bites, he goes into his labyrinths to break the line against the sharp rocks and the barnacles. You have to have patience, feel his twisting path, in order to get him out. But like the tramboyo's labyrinths, the paths in El Patillo Ahogado are very treacherous. You have to learn not to look down where you put your feet. You have to feel with your heart the play of the water, the roundness of the stones, the noise of the sun when it is strong. The eyes, the ears, the feet—all of them have to learn from the heart. You hold there, steady, with the tramboyo on the line, for an hour or two. Jumping here, running there. You learn a lot.

When Lalo learned to walk in El Patillo Ahogado as if he were walking on any other beach, he was ready to learn to fish in Tancay. Because fishing with people is hard, Alejandro. Even more so with people who are always asking questions, like you. . . . Lalo had to learn to remain patient in front of others, which is not easy. Because with other people one changes. We always want to stand out. Impress. Switch places. So when the fish were really biting, I would tell him to stop fishing, to sit down and watch us. Because control does not come from the senses; it comes from inside us. The Good Fisherman casts his line when he feels good inside, not when others' hooks are full.

Without control, one becomes mesmerized by the ocean. You step on your lines. You become envious. You pay attention to other people's lines, but you do not feel your own. When you have control, none of that bothers you. Then you can hear the humming of the line in the wind or under the water. You feel the hook brushing against the snails. You do not feel that the others are winning. That feeling is an illusion. You should never covet what belongs to others or even what you share with them. All that is an illusion. . . . You should not desire things too much, or you could even lose your life, like the gringo Hermelindo. Isn't that so, Alejandro?

In any case, long after he had begun, Lalo learned to fish on La Pared. To complete his training. To know himself completely. Because on La Pared Lalo had to conquer a different fear. In reality, it is a desire that comes dressed as fear. That is the enemy there. The wind, the sun, the pull of the chita—those are nothing. You have to conquer the desire to jump. It is a fear that comes from the very root of your hair. It is a dark fear that we always feel, but that on the precipice grows stronger.

At first, Lalo would follow me to La Pared only for a short while. He had to look around. Over there! At the gray mountains. At El Dorado, our great *apu*, our mountain god. Or else over there! Samanco. All white. Brilliant. You look around. Only later, very slowly, you learn to look down. The black rocks. The white foam. The green waves. The extremely slow snails. . . . Otherwise, the water makes a pact with your fear and mesmerizes you; it pulls you in. The water calls. If you do not have control, if your heart is not clean, you obey. But when you have conquered the desires dressed as fear, then you can look at the clouds, at the playful birds. Then you say to yourself, "How beautiful the world is! Thank you, apu! It is beautiful to be a fisherman!"

16
The Sitios

There are good sitios and there are bad sitios, Alejandro. I think this backyard is a good sitio, for example. It loosens the tongue. It helps the memory. The bluish moon hides the wrinkles and the other pains drawn on the face. Like young lads we are. The soft breeze that plays with the sand dust seems to be touching the soul. It is no longer so painful to revisit the past. . . . Just as it is for remembrance, so it is for fishing. We would have to say that there are good sitios and bad sitios in which to grasp the meaning of the nature of things, of their way of being. . . .

In Tancay you had to look for a good sitio every day. There were preferred sitios, of course, but they were not reserved. The fish did not tell you where they were going to be the next day! Not like us. Genaro says that we humans are easy to predict. He says that he knows half the world since he set up his muffler shop on Avenida Victor Raul Haya de la Torre. . . . If only we could have at least predicted what was going to happen to you. . . . We would have done something, perhaps. . . . It is not so easy with fish, Alejandro. You had to negotiate your sitio every morning.

The Good Fisherman had to be flexible, like the fish. He had to be on the move all the time, from rock to rock, from beach to beach. Of course, not everything was without rhyme or reason. There were ways to handle things. One put experience to good use. For example, a sitio on La Punta was worthless on winter afternoons when the wind whistled loudly and the drops of water rose up to the clouds. It seemed like it rained all the time. And a sitio on La Pared was worthless on summer afternoons, when the sunlight shone even on the black rocks. The whole world then became flat and smooth and shimmered like the desert at midday.

Let us not forget that the Good Fisherman was always aware of what was happening around him. He would sense his companions. When he found a good sitio, he would let them know with signals. Because the Good Fisherman would never monopolize the sitio; he was not greedy. On the contrary: he would make room for others; his line would be laid right at his feet; the twirling of his sinker would be controlled; he would not cross the lines of the others. The Good Fisherman knew respect. And if for any reason he had to leave his sitio, the Good Fisherman would roll up his line, pick up his things, and leave it once and for all. He would not reclaim the sitio unless it was abandoned.

Yes, Alejandro, there are sitios that are good, and there are sitios that are bad. Everywhere. There are sitios that connect us with the whole world in an instant. There are sitios that make us jumpy, almost as if we were trying to sleep with our eyes open. And there are good sitios and bad sitios for every single thing. Los Gentiles knew how to recognize good sitios for planting, for building houses, for having children, for burying the dead. . . .

The bad thing about the city is that here it seems as though all the sitios, good and bad, are disappearing; it seems like the world is shrinking. People seem to be walking around not finding a way to connect with it. With each new dawn it seems everything is becoming the same: flat, smooth, as when the sun hits La Pared on summer afternoons. . . .

But no, Alejandro, do not worry; even in the city there are good sitios and bad sitios. You only have to know how to find them. Genaro knows; he has found a good sitio on Avenida Victor Raul Haya de la Torre. . . . It was good for something because that is where we received the news of your final return. . . . Be that as it may, Alejandro, I can only tell you that Genaro never tires of saying that he was waiting for you. . . . But that is how he is, enigmatic. . . . As for me, I did not even have an inkling that you had returned. God only knows why. . . .

17
Words

You must be getting bored. You must have realized by now that I was not born to be a storyteller. And it is the first time I have set out to recapture the past in this way. I always refuse. "Find someone else," I say. That is why it is doña Pelagia who almost always tells the stories. Only this time she refused first: "It is your turn, Morales," she told me, as if she were a platoon leader. "It is the right thing. I saw him only from afar. And the poor boy is going to need a lot in order to come back to dance with the sun." That is what she said to me. And when doña Pelagia refuses, there is no way to make her change her mind. One has to do things her way. That is why you must be bored. It is difficult to unravel what is cloudy in my memory. One has to have a gift for that. I must be leaving out too much. But it comforts me that the night is blue. . . . Let us go on. . . .

And I should tell you that we, too, liked to laugh. What do you think? We liked to tell jokes. But, most of all, we liked to talk about life. Because there was a lot to laugh about there. For example, the story about the snakes that Ricardo took to the jungle is very funny. . . . I will tell it to you later. Now let us finish with the fishermen. . . . Of course, we used to laugh and tell stories. Our voices played with the wind. Genaro says that our words could be heard all the way to the Pan American Highway. I think it was more likely that he had good hearing.

We would never talk when we were fishing. There, you really had to concentrate. You had to feel the fish in the silence because the human voice is disconcerting. You always have to pay attention to it. Las Almitas, La Piedra, Los Gentiles, El Rey—they all warned about danger with words. You had to be alert. Besides, it is not good to talk to people without looking them in the eye. It is disrespectful. And that is distracting. That is why you were a handful. Jumping. Running. Yelling . . . but we did come to miss you. When you left, there were deep holes, raw silences, everywhere. Until you returned to stay with us . . .

The sound of the waves, of the wind, of the light itself, helped concentration. The sound of the ocean made us feel calm inside. Thinking about it, remembering it, we could lighten our lives, even if we were far from Tancay. It must be because those sounds turn the world dense, solid. They make it endure. The flat silence, the hummingbird hum of the desert did not affect us much when we were there. But it is different here in Chimbote, the city. I think doña Pelagia is right when she says that that's what's in the tar and the cement: desert silence.

When I was a little boy, my father took me to the river. To that river that I told you came down by San Jacinto, turbulent from time to time. A river on the edge of the desert. Where Los Gentiles walk. With lots of *retama* and junco bushes to hide in. With flitting shadows that dance at midday. . . . I had never seen so much water in one place, Alejandro. It came tumbling, laughing, as they say that the waters come down from the highlands.

My father lowered me to a round, flat rock near the foam and told me to listen to the voice of the river. "There are those who understand what the waters say," he told me. "To do that one has to quiet his heart. With peace within you, you can understand the secrets of life, of the world."

I had no idea then that I would come to Tancay. But yes, I did learn a little of what those cold waters were saying. Walking along those beaches, I learned something about life, about the world. I grew inside . . . but maybe it is not the same as understanding the river, Alejandro, because, as we have already said, each thing has its own way of being. This modern world, as it is called, has different sounds, for example. But they, too, have their own way. You only have to unravel the mystery of their nature.

That must be why Genaro looked for the noisiest sitio he could find, fixing mufflers. Before, when Tancay was just beginning to sink into our memory, he had begun to sell tomatoes. "To learn the sound of the marketplace," he told me. I think he could not stand so much murmuring. Because in the marketplace of the city, voices really do mingle together. . . .

That is how it is, Alejandro. There seems to be no way out. I will soon have to look for a new sitio. What will I become? Perhaps I will become a storyteller and go out into the streets of Chimbote to tell truths and follies. Perhaps I will end up like you. . . .

18
Las Almitas

Seeing things in their proper light, every beginning and every end must have its own reason for being. The thing is that often those reasons are wrapped in darkness. That is why we must remember from the beginning, polishing and polishing our memories; we would not want to lose sight of something that you might need in order to return to dance with the sun. As for me, I always like to start from the beginning because that way I can see the meaning of life a little clearer and thus find the courage to keep afloat. That is why, as if we were Good Fishermen, we must stand firm, Alejandro. . . . That is why we have to remember Las Almitas of Tancay.

You might not have noticed them because you did not have eyes for such things. But we did; we knew that Las Almitas walked among the rocks. Most of them appeared wrapped in the morning mist or in the afternoon shadows, when the men were already tired of looking at the sky, at the desert, or at the ocean. They were the spirits of those who died hundreds or thousands of years ago. Because not everyone goes away in a single breath and completely, as the priests say. Some of us remain among these mountains and alleyways, retracing our steps, rehearsing excuses, looking for someone who can tell us something about our past so that we can find our way again. . . .

We had known several *almitas* when they still nestled within the living. Like the ghost of Paulo, for example—the dark-skinned twin who died of grief in his homeland and who returned to Tancay to suffer for who knows how long. He would appear at all hours, looking at his hands in a daze. When the moon was full, the poor soul would look far out to sea and talk to the shadows of the waves. Genaro says that when the wind blew softly, Paulo could be heard praying for his brother. . . . Hermelindo also suffered in Tancay. He would appear running along the shore of the beach when the afterglow of the sun faded away. He would go along throwing fish into the ocean. One by one. When the moon was full, we could see his blond hair fluttering in the wind. The ocean would give him back all his fish. But he would go on: back and forth, back and forth.

At times Las Almitas appeared wearing disguises so that one would think they were just people doing ordinary things in the world. Some might have been full of loneliness and were only looking for a way to pass the time. But others, older and more savvy, wanted to pull us into their world so we would take their place, and they could go on to heaven or hell. There must be nothing worse than walking around like them, dragging their feet, suspended for thousands of years, without being able to do anything but watch people being happy or sad.

Sometimes they appeared dressed as women. They wore long dresses that floated in the air. They asked for help, saying that their husbands had just fallen into the water and were drowning. You would go to see and bam! they would push you in. Many have died that way. At other times they appeared as beautiful women dressed in white cotton nightgowns and long veils covering their faces. You could see the form of their bodies, of their breasts, of their pubic hair. Sometimes they let you see their white teeth, their rosy lips, their eyes black as night. They were beautiful. Genaro used to tell us that if we were to see them as clearly as that, it was best to think about the worst thing we could: the death of our mother, the sores on a friend's back. It was the only way to escape their bewitching.

At times they appeared as gringo children playing in the foam. Those were Los Duendes, the souls of those who died too young to be wicked, but too old to be without sin. What must they have done in life to suffer like that. They were beautiful. They cried with such feeling. They pleaded. "Come, dear friend," they would say. Their eyes were like pools of pure milk. If you were to see them without warning, you wanted to go with them into the water. Once there, the duende would jump on your back and take you away. . . . Many were tempted that way. The best you could do in such cases was to calm yourself, look three times to the top of a mountain, and return your gaze to the foam. Almost always by then they would have disappeared. But if they were still there, then you had to cry out like a newborn baby because it was your soul that wanted to go to the foam; it wanted to get lost in that world. That is how it was, Alejandro; Los Duendes waited for our own souls to betray us.

As I was telling you, some of those almitas were good and were only looking for company, like anyone who had been away from people for thousands of years would do. Don't you think so, Alejandro? They did not want to hurt anybody. Sometimes they even saved our lives. As happened with me during the earthquake of '70. . . . What? You don't think that I, too, could need saving? Sooner or later we all are going to need something or someone, Alejandro. Remember that so that you will not become impatient with us. I will tell you what happened to me so you can see. . . .

I remember that I was thinking I should have gone to watch the soccer game, like everyone in Villa María, because it was Mother's Day, and in those days we used to organize great soccer matches. . . . But I needed money. I had promised to buy a dress for my Aurora. "What better way to spend Mother's Day?" I thought to give myself courage.

In any case, I was catching chita in La Punta. And not very small ones. With day-old langostino, no less. When, all of a sudden, I noticed that something strange was happening with the world. The clouds were zooming by, and the wind swirled, not knowing which way to go. Even the water seemed spooked. Seeing all that, I felt a deep chill, as if from a nameless fear. Just then, from behind the big crag, I heard a voice: "You already have lots of fish," it said to me. "Why don't you go home and give them to your wife?" The voice came to me as in an early-morning dream, one of those dreams that come when you are between waking and sleeping. I did not recognize the voice. To overcome my fear, I told myself that it must be the practical joke of a mischievous fisherman who was passing by, and I kept on fishing.

Then, the voice came even more clearly: "Go home! You already

73

have enough!" it said, almost angry. So I left La Punta to see who this fool was. And just as I was reaching the little path high up on the mountain, I saw a white form that seemed to float over a flat rock. It looked like a huge woman wrapped in swirling veils. And I tell you that suddenly, I don't know why, I felt like going to see if my lunch was where I had left it. I was not even afraid. Very strange, *caramba!*

So I ran to the right, to where the mountain meets the beach. And then, as soon as my feet touched sand, the earth began to shake. The rocks began to dance all over the place like maruchas trapped in a caito. Blue and red rocks came rolling down everywhere. La Punta, where I had been, was like a baby's rattle. It seemed like the world was coming to an end, Alejandro. Not even the birds seemed to be out of danger. They crashed into one another, as if they were drunk. I do not know if you would remember, but that earthquake lasted a long time—an eternity. When it ended, all of Tancay was covered in a pink dust.

Then, as if to put an exclamation point on things, a huge rock began rolling down from the very top of the mountain. It came down enveloped in a cloud of golden dust that under the swaying sun seemed to glitter. It leveled out its own path, rolled out to La Punta, and then, as if alive, seemed to want to go back up. Damn. It seemed to be trying to decide whether to go back up the mountain or to fall on its side. It must have decided on that because it fell to its left with a thump. . . . Someday, when you come back to Tancay, you will see that the poor thing is still there; only now it seems as though it has been lying there since the beginning of time.

I came back to Villa María as best I could. Trembling. With the earth still shaking from time to time, as if it had a fever. When I was passing by the summer camp, I had a strong urge to look back. There was the form, floating over La Punta. And so I blessed myself with the sign of the cross three times and thanked it for saving my life. The form read my thoughts. It made me feel calm inside. . . . I think it was one of Los Gentiles doing me another favor. . . . Then farther on, I looked at the face of La Piedra, just in case. She remained serene, unperturbed. Not at all like what happened with us humans. Because you must know that our lives were embittered on account of that earthquake. . . .

But there are also almitas who are very happy to come and go between what is up and what is down, Alejandro. They are the ones who once nestled within good people who suffered heinous acts. Mistrustful. Lost. Foundered. They come out from the shadows, little by little, following the sound of their names and the threads of the memory of those who loved them in life. At first they come out to retrace their steps only on blue nights, like this one. They go back quickly to their sitios. Then later they walk at dawn or at dusk. They begin to get used to the light. Until one day they find their path and go straight up to heaven. There they rest. They look at our world with pity. But they never forget us. They return, Alejandro. We can see them, clearly, dancing in the sunlight, quivering in the depths of our memory. They bring joy to our lives, Alejandro. They give us hope. They help us to clean our hearts. This we know. Since the beginning of time . . .

19
Viroca

Doña Pelagia is fluttering against the light of her candles. I wonder what the old lady is saying. . . . But do not worry, Alejandro. Let us go on remembering. Repeating, rather, which is how one remembers best. My body is a little finicky: it eases and it aches when it wants to. If only memories were engraved in the body, as Genaro says! But that can't be; the things of the past can never be seen as clearly as you can feel the aches of the body. As times passes, it fades, Alejandro, like the tramboyo in its labyrinths. Will Las Almitas still be wandering about in Tancay, for example, now that there are no people to keep them company? Perhaps they are fading away, too, like everything we were and saw there. The only thing that might remain of them will be our trimmed memories. . . . But that can't be, right?

Even if you have lived it all, there are always silences, misunderstandings, even lies in remembering. Sometimes we lie to ourselves on purpose. But we lie to ourselves mostly without knowing it. That is why the past has many faces, many ways of nestling in the present. You cannot remember things as if you were reading, like the priests believe, as if words could overcome time. Words are only an echo, Alejandro. It is better to listen to several ways of saying the same thing. In all that noise maybe a little of what was can be found. . . . Perhaps that might help us to understand the story of Viroca, the rock-and-roll star. Here is his story.

When Villa María was born in the desert, El Rey de la Mojarrilla built his house on a wide street. There he fenced in a corral. The people of Villa María knew him feeding his animals and taking his

77

children to the beach so they could get some fresh air. In those days the damn factories had not yet ruined everything, and one could still open one's lungs without fear. In time, his daughters embraced their mother's world and left the waves and the rocks to the boy. Everything seemed normal.

But in reality something was twisted. One blindingly hot day doña Dorotea, the mother, noticed that one of the boy's eyes had veered to the left. . . . It was a terrible shock. . . . With the grief for having such bad luck, the mother accused El Rey of having left the boy alone, near Los Duendes. The poor thing must have seen them from the corner of his eye, she thought. Los Duendes do not want to be seen by innocent children because the children remind them of what they have lost, so they probably threw him the bad wind. And to compound the misfortune, there was no one in Chimbote who knew how to straighten eyes twisted by the bad wind.

Knowing that the mother was worried and hurt, El Rey endured her words and said nothing. To console her, he took his son all the way to Catacaos in search of a cure. But all the healers in those lands told him the same thing: the ailment had no cure because it was part of his very being. The boy was born to be different from the rest. . . . It seems that was how things began. Always witty and alert to other people's misfortunes, the fishermen gave him a nickname: Viroca, the "One with the Veering Eye." From then on the boy's true name was lost in the labyrinths of memory.

Some say that when Viroca was little, he used to go with his mother to gather seaweed and catch hairy crabs at El Dorado. Others say that the boy never really knew other rocks than those of Tancay. Genaro says that Viroca knew how to stand in the waves like a crabber. But this much is certain: we all remember that he liked to sing. And he did not sing *huaynos* and *tonderos*, as would be expected of the son of El Rey. He would sing merengues, *cumbias*, and most of all rock and roll, as it is called. The thing is, he used to walk about the desert rocking to strange rhythms. He must have felt different inside, perhaps. But in any case . . . when Viroca grew up, he began to go with his father to the pier at Besique. There he learned how to fish. El Rey gave him an old line, a hook, and bait and left him alone. "A chip off the old block," the fishermen would say because Viroca had a knack for fishing.

Everything went well for several years—until, as any good father nowadays, El Rey had to accept the world of books and clocks and sent Viroca to the new school in Villa María. This must have been around the days when you arrived. But I am sure you do not remember him. You went around annoying everybody with your questions, and he was still just an ordinary little boy. . . .

If you could have seen him on the first day of class! Viroca left his house transformed into a real schoolboy: without a grain of sand in his hair, with a white smock that had long ties, and with a pair of black shoes that made him float over the dust of Villa María like a sparrow in springtime. And to top it off, he carried his school supplies in a white and red bag, the Peruvian colors, made by his mother because, as everybody knew, from the very beginning doña Dorotea wanted Viroca to rise above his misfortune through education.

But such is life; man makes plans, but it is God who decides. In the very first days it was crystal clear that Viroca would never become a good student. On the contrary. He cried like a caged cat. And as soon as he finished his classes, instead of going to play soccer like all the other boys in the barriada, he would run to Tancay to sing and to fish. Maybe it was for having heard Viroca so much or maybe out of respect for El Rey, but the thing is that we got used to his singing. We welcomed him. In those days no one took notice that, in reality, Viroca was not interested in the sea, that he used to go to Tancay only because he liked to sing into the wind and the waves.

You must remember, too, that in those days El Rey still had hopes that Viroca would become a Good Fisherman. Because, I tell you, the boy caught fish nonchalantly, as if he were accepting a well-deserved gift. The fishermen used to advise him to learn as Lalo did instead of relying on luck. Because we know that luck is only luck; it always comes in pairs, good and bad. But Viroca was not interested in those things. He would come and go singing. He was the only one who could sing and fish at the same time without making our lives miserable.

20
The Rock-and-Roll Star

When Viroca finished primary school, discord came to his home. El Rey had already accepted fate and even wanted the boy to leave school and go fishing with him. But doña Dorotea insisted that Viroca continue with his books. And the discord lasted for weeks. The neighbors in Villa María heard the fights at all hours . . . until one day doña Dorotea, in a moment when she put her soul into it, threatened to sell the milking cow and move back to her homeland. . . . Seeing such determination, El Rey could do nothing but accept his wife's decision. That is why Viroca continued in school; that is how he came to develop his vocation as a singer. It was in high school that he began to wear dark glasses and shirts with high red collars.

It must be said, Alejandro, that Viroca did not announce that he was going to be a singer until the December of his graduation, somewhere around '85, the same year that you came dressed like a woman. But when he did it, he did it with such pizzazz that we have something to remember.

Since it was the first graduating class of the barriada, all of Villa María was there. Don Franco, the director, had asked Viroca to premiere the school anthem. He sang so beautifully, I tell you, Alejandro, that even the young men wept. El Rey had to control himself to avoid making a scene.

When Viroca finished, a long silence, like in a dream, resounded in the school. And it was in that silence that Viroca announced his determination to form a musical group. As expected, the people shouted with joy: "Hurray! Hurray! Hurray!" Only then, so as not to hear the chanting, did El Rey put his face in his hands and let his tears fall. It was then known for sure that Viroca would never become a Good Fisherman.

Doña Dorotea saw everything from outside. She had arrived at the school early, but she did not want to sit with the others. She was a little strange. But when the students applauded like at a soccer game, doña Dorotea pushed herself to the middle of the hall, pointed at her son, and told him to stop such foolishness. I tell you that she seemed possessed by forces greater than anger or bitterness. Planted there, floating in the silence trapped between the walls, doña Dorotea looked at her son from head to toe. Something awful was about to happen. The people held their breath. Then, when an eternity had passed, as if something had unknotted in her heart, doña Dorotea embraced her son, and she, too, wept. . . . Ah, destiny, Alejandro! God only knows what misfortune we escaped that day. And God only knows what part that unknotting of the heart played in the fabric of misfortune that came afterwards. . . .

In the hot days of January that followed, Viroca set out to catch chita on La Punta. He fished as if favored by Los Gentiles. And when it seemed that luck was beginning to abandon him, he left the rocks once and for all. He hooked up with three other guys from Chimbote, bought two red drums, an electric guitar, and a Japanese record player. That is how he began to make money. He would play records and accompany them with the guitar and the drums. Later he put the record player aside. But he always wore dark glasses and high red collars. . . . This is the Viroca you must remember because that is how he appeared on television, one week before you went back to the highlands, shortly before Canchero sent his dogs to soil everything. Don't you remember? Let us look for the meaning, the way of being of your memories, Alejandro. Do not embitter your heart. . . .

Doña Pelagia says that El Rey left Villa María a long time ago. She says that the earthquake, the tidal wave, and the mudslide finished off any sign of his house and his backyard. Several years ago now she told me that one of El Rey's daughters, Gabriela, had gone to Lima to try her luck as a model on television. Who knows how she fared. The other daughter, Teresa, went off after a very tall gringo, a member of the Peace Corps, to a faraway place called Colorado because all the mountains are red. Once there, she married another man, also a gringo, who they say makes his living selling futures. I wonder what that is. Of those things I truly don't know anything. There is so much that one does not know. . . .

If you were to ask Lalo, he would tell you that Viroca was his only friend in Tancay. Because they were like brothers. They understood each other. But since Viroca became a singer, they stopped seeing each other. The other day, when Lalo was here, he told me that Viroca is no longer Viroca, but Mike Muñoz, or MM. It seems he has abandoned the dark glasses and the red collars as well. Now he play castanets, recites strange poems, and has spiked green hair. Poor guy. Genaro says that he hears him from time to time. In his dreams. He says that Viroca's song is disjointed and sad. . . .

21
The Wells

You remember that in Tancay we always kept our sitios clean. Old bait worms: to the water. A discarded tin can: to the watchman. Plastic dancing in the wind: to the trash. . . . Because it is not only the heart that must be kept clean, Alejandro, but the rest of the world as well. The cleanliness of one is worthless, it does not last, without the cleanliness of the other. That is something that many people, like Canchero, for example, never understand. They start the destruction from both sides.

But neither can one do a good cleaning just for the heck of it. Don't you think? To clean well you have to keep in mind that it is something good for life. And it is worse yet if one cleans up only to please someone else, even if it is God. That is not good because it does not last. It is better to clean the heart and the world, keeping in mind our own pleasures and desires, knowing that what goes around, comes around. Because the world turns, Alejandro, and in the end we meet up with our own footprints. Do you understand? The world turns. That is why it is never good to say: "Of this water I shall never drink."

I do not know if I am making myself understood. Sometimes I feel that I lack the words, that I leave out too much. So maybe it would help if I tell you the story that doña Pelagia told me. Because she really comes up with the perfect stories and as if from nowhere. Although she does not like to tell stories. If only you were to stay around here a few more years, she would surely tell you her stories. Because she really likes you. Who knows why. Sometimes she takes a liking to people and things without rhyme or reason. However, I warn you, sometimes her stories are confusing. They are long and bear the weight of ancient times. . . . Let us see if with her words you understand me. . . .

A long time ago, in the time of Los Gentiles, before the Spaniards arrived here, the king of all the Incas wanted to know if there were rich people in these parts. Since his wishes were law, he asked his people to send to Cusco the three best men to satisfy his curiosity. "Send me the three best," he said. "The one who finds what I want will be general of my army and will govern those lands in my name." Since the Incas were obedient, they found the three best men and sent them to Cusco.

The first man arrived from the south. He came with a beautiful llama and a poncho made of fine alpaca. Right then and there one could see that he was good. The second one came from the east. He walked beside a strong guanaco and wore a poncho made of vicuña. Right then and there one could see that he also was good. The third one came from the north. He arrived on foot and wore a poncho made of cotton. Seeing them in the grand plaza of Cusco, the king told them: "Go to the northern coasts where the waters are teeming with fish and bring me proof that there are rich people there." And so the three men left Cusco.

They walked days and nights together. They climbed up and down high snow-capped mountains; they crossed turbulent rivers and green valleys; they roamed through red deserts. When they had walked many days and nights, they arrived at the edge of these deserts. They had never seen sand so clean, so yellow. They thought that perhaps this was the sea about which their king had spoken. But when they touched it with the tips of their toes, they realized that it was not water. So they sat there, not knowing what to do.

They stayed sitting at the edge of the desert for days and nights. But by then the king of these lands already knew that the three men had arrived. His advisors, who were very wise, knew also why they had come. So the king, who was wiser than all of them, told his advisors: "Send them messengers to show them the three paths that lead to Chan Chan." And so it was done.

The messengers found the travelers still sitting at the edge of the desert. So they said to them: "This is called desert. It is like the sea, except that it is hot. If you want to get to where you are going, you have to cross it. There are only three paths that lead to where you want to go. The first is short but hot like fire. The second is longer, but only as hot as a pot near the fire. The third is longer still, but only as hot as the sands where you are sitting." And they asked the travelers to choose.

The man with the llama chose the shortest path. He thought that since he could carry all the water he wanted, he could arrive at Chan Chan faster. The man with the guanaco chose the second path. Since he had a smaller animal, he thought he could carry less water. The man who came on foot chose the longest path. And so they entered the desert.

They walked days and nights. After walking a long way, they found themselves without water and lost in the desert. Seeing their misfortune, the king of these lands sent his messengers so they could show each man a well of water. And so they did. "What?" the messengers said, dragging the men to their water wells, "You did not know where this little well was?" And they disappeared. The men drank all the water they could. Then they filled their gourds.

And so it was that the man with the llama came to think that perhaps his well was the only one in all the desert. He thought that maybe he had been the only one chosen by the gods to be saved from certain death. And then he got the idea to spoil the well so that no one else could drink from it. So he pulled down his pants and soiled the freshwater. He took his gourds and left.

The man with the guanaco had almost the same idea. Thinking himself already the governor, he buried the water well so that the others could not find it. He filled it with hot sand, level with the desert; then he took his gourds and left.

Drinking the freshwater, the man dressed in cotton thought that perhaps the others would also be thirsty. Besides, since he could not carry much water, he thought that maybe he would have to return to the little well sooner or later. And so he cleaned his water well, took his gourds, and left, . . .

22

The King of Chan Chan

Once again the men walked through the desert for days and nights. Until they had drunk all their water. When they were about to die of thirst, the messengers reappeared and took them to their wells. The man with the llama realized that it was the same well that he had soiled. It was full of worms. Since he was dying of thirst, he tried to drink the water anyway. But the worms clung to his lips, to his face. That was how the man with the llama died, looking at worms.

When the man with the guanaco arrived at the place of his well, it was no longer there. Then he realized that it was the same one he had buried. Dying of thirst, he tried to dig out the little well with his bare hands. He could almost smell the water, just a little bit lower, but it was too late. The man with the guanaco also died of thirst in the desert.

The man dressed in cotton drank of the freshwater. Looking around for the others, he filled his gourds. Not seeing them, he began to walk again. This time, after walking for a long time, he arrived at the center of Chan Chan. They received him well, and he was grateful for the welcome. "Your companions died of thirst," the king of Chan Chan told him. "They never learned to keep their wells clean. They could have been good warriors, but never good rulers."

In spite of his fatigue, the man from the north realized that he was speaking with a wise man. He wanted to return to Cusco immediately; he wanted to tell his king that, yes, there were rich and wise people in these lands. But he was too tired to make the trip. So the king of these lands commanded that he be taken to one of his comfortable interior chambers. The man fell asleep there for days and nights. . . .

Many things happened while the man from the north slept. Not having received news, the king of the Incas gathered his powerful army and came over those mountains to conquer these lands. He crossed all the deserts with his caravans of llamas. When he arrived at Chan Chan, he put it under siege. After twelve years of continual battles, the Inca army conquered the Chan Chan people.

When the Inca king had won the last battle, he began to destroy all the wealth, the knowledge, and the wisdom that existed in these lands. He wanted to disintegrate Chan Chan into the desert. He wanted to soil, to bury, and to flatten the people of Chan Chan, like the men with the llama and the guanaco had done with their wells. He must have thought that these people were worthless. . . .

Years went by, until one day, when the Inca governor of Chan Chan was destroying the interior chambers of the great walled city, they found the man dressed in cotton. He was still sleeping. They called him. They shook him. The healers gave him potions. Nothing. The man went on sleeping. And so they brought him to Cusco. There the man continued to sleep for days and nights.

When the man from the north finally woke up, he felt disoriented. He found himself old, surrounded by smells and sounds of a place that he only remembered as if in a dream. "I have slept too much," he said to himself, and suddenly he remembered his mission. He wanted to get up and run to Cusco and tell his king what he had learned on his long journey. But he realized that he was too weak, that his body could not follow his wishes. Moreover, he could not remember much. And so the man from the north stayed in his bed with a heavy heart.

Meanwhile, the Inca king who had sent him to the desert had died. The Inca empire had suffered the consequences of a war between brothers. Atahualpa, the usurper, was king of a bloodstained land. . . . Nevertheless, as soon as Atahualpa knew that the man from the north had awakened, he ran to his deathbed to ask him what had happened. Did he have perhaps a message from the other world?

With his last breath the man from the north told him: "There is only one way to cross the desert, one way to live and to govern: you have to keep your wells clean." And he died.

Doña Pelagia says that maybe if the man dressed in cotton had returned to Cusco, Peru's destiny would have been different. Perhaps the old king would have understood the message and would not have destroyed the people of these lands. But that is life; they destroyed everything. And now?

Well, it so happened that shortly after the man from the north died, Atahualpa was captured by the Spaniards. And when the powerful king was a prisoner, when he was suffering, he asked for help from the people of Chan Chan: "Help me to defend my empire. Help me to get rid of these bearded men riding on fire-breathing beasts. Help me to gather gold and silver to placate their desires." But then the people of Chan Chan did not hear him. The armies from these lands had already been destroyed.

The Inca king had soiled his own wells. He never learned how to live well, much less how to govern well. It is for that reason that these deserts were conquered by people who had never heard the wisdom of the man from the north. That is why the Incas themselves were conquered. That is why we are who we are.

That is why, Alejandro, we should never say, "Of this water I shall never drink." We must keep the world clean because it is here where we must live, until we find a way out or lose ourselves in time. It is not for someone else that we must clean the world and our hearts. No. It is for ourselves. . . .

But, frankly, I do not know if doña Pelagia's story says that. Sometimes she says very strange things. Genaro swears that when they begin to tell stories, she always comes out ahead because she lengthens them, shortens them, gives them endings and beginnings as she pleases. She must know a lot, perhaps. Don't you think? That is why I follow her advice: "Go out to the backyard so you can remember with Alejandro." "Very well, Pelagia." Even though, bathed in this bluish light, I am once again feeling that the remembering is giving me wrinkles. . . .

23

Ricardo

Let me stretch, Alejandro, to get the knots out of my body . . . it will not be long now. Doña Pelagia is lighting more candles. There are a lot of people in that dark little parlor she has. You must remember it: plaster saints everywhere, yellow and red geraniums, old nets that look like spider webs. . . . She says she is going to buy a dried swordfish to put in her window next to the blowfish that look like balloons. . . . Must be because she always wanted to fish. . . . That is how it is, Alejandro. Not everyone can become a Good Fisherman . . . even if they want to. Like doña Pelagia, perhaps. Or like you, for example, who arrived searching for something, but not wanting to learn anything. "This way, Alejandro, that way, Alejandro"—nothing; you were like those turtles who beach themselves. There were many people like that. And not all of them went far away, like you, to search for justice, as you said.

But let us leave the sadness aside, even if for just a while. And to do that: let us fulfill what we have promised. Let us talk about Ricardo, to lighten our hearts. You must remember him, Alejandro. It was he who took the funny snakes up to the mountains. . . . He used to go often to Tancay. But, like you, he never became a Good Fisherman. Even before he learned to drive trailer trucks, he always arrived at the rocks looking like he was ready to leave. But, it must be said, whenever he came back, he would bring stories that made us laugh, although sometimes they also made us angry. But there is a lesson in everything. . . .

When Ricardo turned twenty-one, his father, don Sebastián, who had several trailer trucks in Chimbote, gave him one to drive.

That Ricardo! He was as happy as a dolphin in January. He drove that truck everywhere. He would disappear from Tancay for months. Later he would show up, blowing his horn on the Pan American Highway. Sometimes, when the desert wind was blowing soft, we could hear him passing by. . . . And so time went by . . . until don Sebastián's business went from bad to worse, and he had to suspend operations. That is when Ricardo spent a while in Tancay and told us of his experience. Let us see if you like it. . . .

A few months before Ricardo came to the rocks, they asked him to bring an enormous pipe from Chimbote to the mountains in the north, up there where they say that the highlands and jungle meet. "What is this" thought Ricardo, "that I should go all the way up there with a single pipe? Isn't that a waste?" But he did not say anything because it was the very government who was sending him. Besides, he wanted to go to the jungle because in all of his travels he had never been there. So he went with his pipe to the very rim of the Andes, the "eyebrow of the jungle," as they call it.

He traveled up the northern roads, resting and sleeping in his cab. It was all uphill. Summer. The heat was so bad, he says, that he had to wet his hands in a pail of water in order to grasp the steering wheel. The roads were horrible. The bridges were half falling down. Landslides had left deep ruts all over the place, and the dust was like sawdust. The rear tires at times hung over the precipices. On top of it all, Ricardo was afraid that the pipe would roll off. But with the patience of a cordelero, he continued on.

He arrived at the camp on the third day. There he noticed that several pipes of different colors were already piled up on top of some pink rocks. In that camp—which was in a small, damp, flat place—there was a store with a little bar attached to it. Like all the buildings in that place, the little bar was made of yellow reeds and sat on stilts made of stripped poles. . . . Ricardo says that everything is built on stilts there because it rains a lot, that the people walk around afraid that at any minute El Niño will bring its Ecuadorian clouds. It must be like living with the fear of earthquakes, landslides, and repressions. . . . Anyway, a very pretty young girl worked in that little store. Ricardo told us that she had long braids and light-blue eyes, and that she dressed in green day and night. Her name was

Blanca Nieves, Snow White. Imagine that. The thing is that the guy was impressed. . . .

Looking around the place all wide-eyed, Ricardo saw cables, dump trucks, caterpillars, every kind of machinery. The people looked like they were working hard, moving from here to there, carrying things. The dump trucks would cross a muddy plaza, leave their load on the edge of a cliff, and go back for more. "Caramba!" Ricardo said to himself. "The people up here really do earn their pay." When the engineer finally arrived to tell him where to unload his pipe, Ricardo saw that they had a crane ten times bigger than the one that had come to take away La Piedra.

When the crane deposited the pipe on top of the pink rocks, Ricardo felt relieved. He could now return to his coast, where everything is flat—maybe sandy and even dusty, but flat. And he would have turned around right then and there, but he realized that it was late. Because, as I was telling you, the roads in the north are dangerous and treacherous. It was not wise to leave at that hour. Besides, the engineer himself advised Ricardo to stay. So he resigned himself to spend the night in that place. He ate in the little bar. Just bananas and rice! Because he says that up there the people eat bananas every day. They fry them and they boil them as if they were fish!

Afterwards, he took a walk around the camp wherever the ground was dry. It had already been a while since the sun had set, but the sky was still red, as if on fire. In that radiance Ricardo could see for miles. He says that from there the peaks of these mountains look like they are made of gold. He could also hear clearly the voices of people whom he could barely see, far away, way below, on the hillsides. He says that it was beautiful. Not like the coast, but beautiful. . . . When night came, Ricardo climbed up into the cab of his truck and went to sleep.

24

Blanca Nieves

The next day Ricardo got up with the birds. There are all kinds of birds up there, he says. Some look like gigantic bees and buzz along in flocks. Very early in the morning. Others fly sort of sideways, looking backwards. And he says that the woodpeckers are so big that you can hear them working far away, as if they were drillers. But, anyway . . . Ricardo had his coffee in the little bar and went out to look for the engineer. They told him to go to a hut at the edge of the camp, near a mound of black soil. That is how the dirt is up there, he says, black like the night.

The engineer was not there. So Ricardo went on looking for him. He looked everywhere. Here. There. Nothing. As for the workers, they looked like ants making holes. Whistles everywhere. Explosions. He says that the dust would go straight up to the sky, not like here, where as soon as the dust is stirred up, the air grabs it and carries it off in threads or whirlwinds. But, walking around amid so much noise and work, Ricardo felt that something was just not right. Some green dump trucks would bring dirt from one end of the plaza, and some red dump trucks would take it back. And that was not all. A group of workers was painting the pipes in different colors! They looked like giant snakes with golden rings.

Suspecting that something was wrong, Ricardo wanted to leave. So he tried harder to find the engineer. He checked around the pink rocks, the piles of black dirt, among the people, the dogs, the machines, until he found him. The man was watching how the dynamite made the hills tremble. Ricardo approached him and asked him to sign the invoice, but the engineer told him that he had to wait. "Go find a woman and stay here for a few days," the engineer told him. "Don't worry about it." And he also told Ricardo that he could charge overtime because he was waiting for orders.

Of course, Ricardo thought this was not quite right, but it seemed to him that the engineer knew what he was doing. In those years the terrorism had not yet taught us to be suspicious of even our own shadows. Besides, surely the girl with light-blue eyes counted for something, right? So Ricardo stayed one more day. Then he stayed another. And another . . . But, of course, Ricardo did not stop thinking about his father. So on the fourth day he insisted that the engineer sign the invoice. "You are losing money, buddy," the engineer told him, but he signed the paper. Then, finally, Ricardo came flying back. . . . Don Mauricio, the truck driver, says that there is nothing like a trailer truck rolling down from the mountains. You take your life in your hands.

When Ricardo got to Chimbote, he was still worried. He thought that the engineers here were going to ask for an explanation. How could it be? Nearly two weeks to bring a single snake! But nobody said anything. The engineers were in really good moods and only asked him about the people they knew at the camp up in the "eyebrow of the jungle," as they call it.

When Ricardo arrived at his father's house, don Sebastián asked him if everything had gone well. Ricardo wanted to make up a story to cover himself, but he saw that it was better to tell the truth. Smiling, his father told him that everybody was making money with the business of the pipes, that the oleo duct, which is what they call what they were making, was a pipe dream. "Is it true that they are painting the pipes like snakes?" he asked him, dying with laughter. . . .

Ricardo's father was very good at making money off The Government. What did it matter that they were never going to finish the oleo duct, as they call it? As long as someone was making money and there were pictures for the newspapers: a national pride, the Peruvian inventiveness. . . . That is why we never liked politicians. One had to avoid them, Alejandro. But with all that, we did not lose patience and set ourselves out to try to right the world, like you did, which has come to cost us so much. . . .

In any case, do not be angry. Let me finish the story, although it seems like it is not going to lighten our hearts, as I had thought; the telling of it has changed its flavor. . . . Ricardo went back to the place in the eyebrow of the jungle three more times. Each time he stayed a little longer. The last time he stayed about a month. When he came back that time, he brought Blanca Nieves with him, the girl with the light-blue eyes. They now have two little boys. Also with light-blue eyes. Ricardo says that they are going to be truck drivers. For her part, Blanca Nieves still dresses in green. You will see that when she comes in to see you. . . .

They say that is how things are around there, Alejandro. Genaro, who really likes to travel about the world, says that there is no place with more worms than up there. He says that there are worms that fly, some that jump, some that swim, and even some that eat other worms. But, imagine, neither Genaro with his worms nor Ricardo with his mountain peaks of gold wants to stay up there. They are always coming back to these shores. There must be something in these lands, in this desert, in this sky. Maybe it is a good sitio to find our paths. . . .

25
Don Augusto

We have now finally arrived at Villa María, Alejandro. It would be good to remember some of the things that happened in our barriada. In part because its fate is tied to that of Tancay, as is the rest of the valley. In part also because, like the lives of all those who are outside waiting for doña Pelagia to invite them to come in to this little backyard, your life touched its alleyways. Let us hope that you can return someday to dance with the sun, Alejandro; let us hope that you can walk again on its street corners and in its markets. Maybe by then you will still find our footsteps scattered around there. . . . According to Genaro, we will always be wandering through that which remains of what used to be.

Villa María was founded way to the south in order to escape the smell of boiled fish that slept in your hair. It was almost lost in that desert, but it survived and extended even farther south. The church was then at the edge because many thought that it was more needed there. For them, it was like a spiritual fortress in the desert. Because in those days many were still afraid of Los Gentiles; there were already very few left who understood them. Later there came people from all over the world, and together they all forgot about Los Gentiles. Neither fear nor respect was left. Except on rare occasions. Like when La Cabra invoked them.

In a few years the streets of Villa María crisscrossed the desert from the foothills of the mountains to the marshes of Veintisiete de Octubre, which in those years did not yet smell of death. The colectivo stops were just getting established. There were not many cars then. At times, up to twelve passengers had to squeeze into them, one on top of the other. It was in those days that Amador Sinfín built his movie theater. It became his shroud when the earthquake hit. They say that they found him in his bed, clutching a Bible. Because, in spite of appearances, he was an evangelist. You must remember him. He used to let you in for free. And you would write about his movies. Lalo used to read me your words so that I would let him go to the theater. . . . They say Amador was a good man.

People got together in clubs in those days. They were not afraid of gathering. Not like later, when that business of hunting down terrorists began. When that happened, no one would meet with anyone else, as if they all reeked of boiled fish. . . . How nice it would be if all that were ending, Alejandro. But, anyway . . . there were all kinds of clubs. Some for organizing soccer games. Others for people interested in improving their hometowns. Others for playing cards. And there were larger organizations: the Association of Parents of Families, Mothers of Villa María, Pro-School. It was in that bubbling of activity when the talk of the market began.

The general call came on a hot day in March. You should remember because in those days you were still going around with your eyes half open; you were learning something of our customs. . . . The leaders said that we had to make order out of chaos. That is what the notice posted on the street corners said: "We must make order out of chaos." If it sounded nice, it was because it spoke the truth: in those days the markets were scattered all over the place. The persistent blue flies would follow the people and the animals everywhere. Remember that this was before the earthquake, before all the blue flies were killed by the gigantic mosquitoes that arrived with the mudslide.

Moreover, the market on the northern edge was sinking. Puddles of salt water appeared and disappeared with the full moon. So when the meeting was announced, the people were expecting something to be done. As usual, everyone talked a lot. Even doña Eva, La Cabra, spoke. . . . We did not know then that in a few days she would be expelled from Villa María. . . . But I am getting ahead of myself. It seems that it is about time to start looking for a way to end our remembering. The awful thing is that, from here on, as with misfortune, everything is downhill. . . . In any case, because the north of Villa María was sinking, it was decided to build the market to the south.

Very early one Sunday the women of Villa María walked to the southern edge of the desert carrying stakes with red and white ribbons. Once there, they cleared the land of rocks, swept away the scorpions, chased off Los Gentiles with chicha and dancing, and planted their stakes. That is why the market is so big, even now, though it is half abandoned. The women quickly set up their stalls with reed mats, juncos, and eucalyptus poles.

As always, the police came on Monday. They came to say that the desert belonged to the navy and that everybody had to leave. The poor women had to fight in turns. The dust from the scuffle rose up so high that its plumes could be seen from as far away as Samanco. But, thank God, the market stayed. That night the women slept in their stalls, together with their dogs and their children. In the days that followed, the committee sent a letter of petition to the government, asking for an engineer to draw up the official plans for the market. Don Xavier Urquides, the Spanish legal secretary who has his place in the Central Market in Chimbote and whom the committee contracted to write up the letter of petition, used very eloquent words, they say. The people waited weeks wondering what was happening with the petition in Lima. Until the women got tired of sleeping in the desert, shooing owls away. It was then that we decided to make order out of chaos on our own. It was then that we called on don Augusto, the mason, who lived next door to the church.

Some say that don Augusto was skinny and hard of hearing. Others say that he was a fat and dark-skinned man from the jungle. Many remember him as stout and missing three fingers on his right hand. Doña Pelagia insists that don Augusto had come from the southern desert because he liked chicha made of peanuts. She also insists that it was don Augusto who built the only walls of the church that did not fall down in the earthquake; that he built, by himself, Amador Sinfín's movie theater, which was why those walls did not fall down; that what killed Amador were the roof rafters that Amador had bought in San Jacinto. . . . Be that as it may, the truth is that don Augusto was called to set up the market because he was already famous for making straight walls without using string or plumb line.

The first thing that don Augusto did was to ask that the desert be cleared of stands and stakes. A band of children did it in the blink of an eye. When everything was clear, he asked for silence, raised his hands to the sky, murmured something, and sat down at the edge of the square piece of desert, near a pile of rocks. There he waited until the sun reached the middle of the sky. Doña Pelagia says that that is how they do things down south, that there are those who can speak with the sun. . . . Suddenly, don Augusto got up, planted a stake at his feet, and raised his gaze to the horizon. His eyes looked like two moons in May. He stayed like that until he had achieved communion, until his heart was clean and the world that was not straight ceased to exist.

Then he began to walk, tracing a line with his left foot. Always looking at the horizon. When he felt that the line was long enough, he stopped. He planted another stake, made a half turn, and began to walk again. Until he had drawn a perfect square. He had not blinked the whole time, and not a single tear had pooled in his eyes. Then he began to trace the interior divisions. The sun had barely moved from its spot when don Augusto finished his work. The people congratulated him, the women began to build their stalls, and the children and the dogs seemed happy for no reason. Ever since then, all the streets in Villa María have been squared by the market. Not long after his feat, don Augusto disappeared from Villa María.

The people say that maybe don Augusto is building other markets down south, because they refuse to believe that he was killed by the earthquake. Many say that they saw him afterwards, talking with the cochos who come once in a while to bask in the sun and to console themselves on the beaches of Veintisiete de Octubre. Others say that it was don Augusto who built the restaurant Los Pinos in the park El Vivero Forestal, that when the new owners of the steel mill began to cut down the eucalyptus trees to make room for cars, he set the whole thing on fire. . . . The fact is that the police looked for him for days. . . . Genaro says, however, that don Augusto went back to his homeland, down south, to a place called Nazca, where the desert is so smooth and so flat that nothing grows and that people can see for kilometers as if they were meters. "He has gone to work for a foreign woman," he told me when we met at La Cocina, looking for *miñoca*, worms for bait. "He is tracing lines for tourists."

The truth is that don Augusto must be old by now. One of these days I am going to go to the south. If I find him, I will give him your regards. Because, although you may not remember now, I know that you held him in high esteem. You used to come with hurried steps to watch him work. He even spoke to you once, and you shook his hand. . . . What a pity it would be, Alejandro, that if by going around with your eyes fixed on the big things, you have lost even the memory of the little ones.

26
Don Mauricio

Do you remember don Mauricio, Alejandro? Maybe not, because he came only occasionally to Tancay. He was a very good friend of Genaro's. I don't know how or why. It seems that they had known each other before, from those lands in the south that Genaro loves so much. Although sometimes Genaro seems to have known the whole world. . . . I wonder . . . But let us pick up the story of don Mauricio so we can continue weaving our memories. That way we can also include something about the earthquake—because, as we were saying, there is a lesson in everything.

To begin his story, I would have to tell you that don Mauricio showed up around here like all the rest: from God knows where. The thing is that he found himself a house in Villa María, and there he planted roots. He lived in his little house until recently. Until doña Serapia, his wife, died of cholera, which came, they say, on Russian ships. When that happened, don Mauricio went to live around San Pedro, near his three daughters, already married and with children. He is still there, but he does not come to the barriada very much anymore. The last time I saw him, his eyes were almost blue from old age, and yet he was still driving a small truck up north. Because in his day, as I told you, don Mauricio was a trucker. . . .

When the earthquake of 1970 shook Chimbote, don Mauricio's truck was loaded with cargo, ready to go. He had already said goodbye to his wife and his three daughters. The shaking caught him at Chong's gas station, filling his tank. All of a sudden, c-r-r-r-ash-bam-boom! Everything was turned upside down, and don Mauricio, like everyone else, wound up crawling on his hands and knees. It was terrible, Alejandro. The shaking seemed endless. People were crawling like drunks all over the place, crying. . . . When don Mauricio could finally straighten up, he left the truck where it was and ran home. He found that his house had fallen as if blown down by a gust of wind. There was not even a place to sit. But, all in all, don Mauricio had to be grateful for his good luck: he found all his family alive and well. They had lost only belongings.

When the earth calmed down, don Mauricio returned to his truck; he had already resigned himself to wait until things passed. No one knew what else to do in those days. So don Mauricio drove the truck to his lot, and when night came, he brought his daughters up to the cab to sleep. He and doña Serapia found shelter under blankets and boxes. They lived like that for several days, cooking and eating on the ground . . . until, like everybody else, they ran out of things. So don Mauricio decided to go to Lima, to bring back something at least. And so about a week after the earthquake don Mauricio got up very early, told his wife and his daughters not to move from their sitio, and left. That is how his man-made misfortunes began, Alejandro.

Don Mauricio told me that he did not have any problems driving on the Pan American Highway, even though there were stretches where the pavement was like a rocky beach. With patience, don Mauricio could negotiate the potholes filled with brackish water, the chunks of cement, the disoriented people. But barely outside of Villa María, don Mauricio realized that our world was changing. Before the earthquake, Villa María had not needed a bridge; now the Lacramarca River had appeared and was raging, signaling the mudslide that was going to come down from the highlands. Before the earthquake, the Pan American Highway did not go over high mounds of sand packed in by the army; now the wind was swirling there like crazy, and people were shivering in the cold, waiting for colectivos. . . . The earthquake changed our lives forever. Don Mauricio told me that on that trip he had the premonition that the shaking of the earth marked the end of Villa María. Perhaps that will be so. As things are going, God knows if all of Chimbote won't become again what it was before we got the notion of making a "Peruvian Pittsburgh," as they say. . . .

Don Mauricio continued ahead. He told me that when he rounded the curve at Besique and saw San Jacinto, his heart was filled with joy: the farmlands were unaffected. There they told him that the people from around those parts had not lost much. Their houses, well made with mud, juncos, and reeds, only danced and frightened the children. But farther to the south, around Casma, it was something else. The city was leveled to the ground. Everything strewn about. Pigs running free. People moaning under the dying *pacay* trees. At the southern end of town, worse yet: the bridge was gone. It had been washed away by the river. Damn! He says it was like the end of the world announced by the evangelists. . . .

With his spirits at their ebb, don Mauricio stopped the truck. How could he go on now? He almost turned around and headed back to Chimbote. But he remembered his three little daughters, without water and without food, and he had no choice but to try to get through by any means. So don Mauricio climbed down from his truck, walked around to feel the pulse of the earth, and squatted down to listen to the flow of the water. For a long time . . .

When don Mauricio had felt and listened enough, he returned to his cab, took out a small shovel, raised a lot of dust, and made a ramp down to the river. Next, he crossed the muddy waters, raised still more dust, and finished the ramp up to the other side. Because that is how he is, Alejandro: extremely patient and tenacious. When he finished his construction, he backed up the eighteen-wheeler, revved up the engine, blew his horn, and drove it into the water.

The poor trailer twisted and creaked going down to the water. The people that were around there fixing their things cheered him on. "Go! Go! Go!" When he got to the other side and went up the embankment, the truck sounded like a sea lion in heat and almost did not make it. But at last it reached the top of the riverbank. It seemed like a miracle . . . but not really—don Mauricio knew that it could be done. As I was telling you, he is a serene man; he knows how to clean his heart. . . . And so he was able to climb the long ascent that they say is there as you are leaving Casma, and he got on the road again, contented.

But then as don Mauricio was rounding the curve of a hill, he heard trucks up ahead coming toward him: it was a convoy of army trucks heading north. The line of covered trucks looked like a green snake slithering up the hill. Don Mauricio was happy, thinking that finally things were going to get better; in his day he had been a sergeant, so he had a lot of respect for everything military. . . . But, unfortunately, that did not help him at all. A Jeep, as they call it, came forward from the convoy, and a soldier got out with his gun in the air to make him stop.

"What's the matter?" asked don Mauricio. The soldier told him that he could not go on. "And why not?" Because those were the soldier's orders: no one could leave Casma without his permission. And immediately he added that he could not give permission on his own. Instead, he ordered don Mauricio to park his truck on the side of the road. They would have to wait for orders.

Of course, don Mauricio was a little angry. What was so bad about going on to Lima? When would the orders come? But, thinking about his little daughters, he was able to clean his heart and decided to wait. And so he sat in his cab and listened to the radio . . . for hours. . . . Meanwhile, the green snake had disappeared out of sight to the north, and there remained only the soldiers with the Jeep. The sun reached the center of the sky, stayed there for quite a while, and continued on. It was so hot, don Mauricio told me, that he saw the soldiers as if they were floating on pink clouds. Because that is what happens in the desert when it is very hot and one begins to lose control. Something awful was about to happen. His heart was telling him so.

27
Lurigancho

After a long time, don Mauricio decided to talk with the soldiers so they would let him go; but they did not pay any attention to him. They told him to stay in his cab until he was told otherwise. Imagine that, Alejandro. Was that maybe why you went off to fight? Was that maybe why we ended up with such misfortunes? Ay, Alejandro; sometimes power is just too powerful. . . . In any case, don Mauricio kept waiting. Until the cab became like an oven and his heart was becoming unclean. Because, as doña Pelagia says, everything has its limits.

When don Mauricio could not take it anymore, he started the motor. The soldiers, who must also have been seeing him float on pink clouds, raised their rifles as a sign for him to turn it off. Being very clever, don Mauricio told them that truck motors had to be warmed up from time to time so they would not break down. Since the soldiers are like us and do not know much about trucks, they let him be.

When the motor was all warmed up, don Mauricio made the sign of the cross on his chest, threw the truck in gear, and gunned it down the highway. Seeing him pass by, the soldiers shot at him, but by now don Mauricio had made up his mind. He had left fear tucked away in some corner of his anger. The soldiers followed him. But don Mauricio says that there is nothing like an eighteen-wheeler going downhill. . . . Maybe the soldiers had orders to stay at their post; maybe, being like us, they had understood his problems. Who knows? The thing is that they let him go.

Don Mauricio ran for several hours along the Pan American Highway. He flew along; because they say that the roads in the south head downhill toward Chile, a long country where the penguins used to come from. On that hot summer afternoon the desert swayed in front of him as if it were a mere illusion. He went on and on downhill until, in a place called Pativilca, still very far from Lima, he came upon a military checkpoint: a barrier across the road. Since his heart was no longer clean, he could not stop. He drove his eighteen-wheeler straight ahead and crashed through the barrier.

The soldiers fired shots at him and drove him off the road into the sand. Don Mauricio was lucky that he was not hurt. Of course, he would have liked to explain things, to tell them about Chimbote and the earthquake. But with all the bitterness choking in his throat, he could not. They handcuffed him and sent him off to Lurigancho, a prison filled with all kinds of criminals. Don Mauricio told me that the prisoners there moan so much that from those cement walls comes a sound like a distant whale.

He stayed in Lurigancho for six months, looking to the north through iron bars made here in Chimbote. He worried about his family, of course, but he knew that we were here. Fortunately. He did not despair. Asking for help from La Piedra, from the Virgin of Chalpón, even from Los Gentiles, he passed the time. He cleaned his heart. He recovered his patience. We did not even know where he was. All we could do was pray for him.

Then, when it seemed that he would stay in Lurigancho for the rest of his life, a guard called his name. They brought him to the warden, a man with a mustache like the movie comic Cantinflas. And that Cantinflas guy said to him, as casually as if he were taking a drink, that don Mauricio was free. No one told him why they were letting him go. Nothing. They just threw him out. Sometimes don Mauricio thinks that it was a miracle from La Piedra. At other times he believes that it was something done by Los Gentiles. Because, he says, on the day he met the Cantinflas guy, there was a strange dawn: it rained with the sun shining, and a bluish rainbow appeared in the middle of some cornfields planted in the form of a cross. One never knows. The fact is that don Mauricio heard the Cantinflas guy, with all his strange mannerisms, as if he were in a movie.

Don Mauricio came back home with no money and without work. His wife was working in don Li's laundry. His oldest daughter, Olga, had become the head of the household and was taking care of her little sisters with the help of the neighbors. Everyone had helped. And they were never without fish to eat. Never. . . . Of course, since don Mauricio still had a bit of fishing line and some hooks, he came to fish at Tancay. There, among the rocks, he completed the cleansing of his heart. There, watching the foam, feeling the deep sound of the sea, telling us his story, he regained his equilibrium. But there as well, with the wind perhaps, his eyes began to turn bluish, like the rainbow in Lurigancho. . . .

That is how things were in the days after the earthquake, Alejandro. Everything seemed to be upside down. People did things they had never done before and would never do again. Because that is what happens with an earthquake; it shakes up not only what you can see, but also the invisible fibers of the heart and of destiny. There are many who still have not regained their equilibrium. There are many who still have no trust in the world. Nothing seems solid to them, long lasting. Maybe it is because they put too much trust in things. It is not good to be too attached to things, Alejandro. Putting things in their proper light, earthquakes teach us how to live. To live through an earthquake is to have seen death out of the corner of your eye. We realize the true value of our daily chores, our preoccupations, our hatreds, our loves, everything. . . . Too bad that by then you were no longer here, Alejandro. Genaro says that we will not have another earthquake for a long time.

28
Don Franco

Of course, it is not only from earthquakes that we can learn. We can learn about life from any one of its aspects, from all kinds of things, and from all kinds of people. I believe that a Good Fisherman knows as much as a good lawyer or a good doctor. The thing is that what each one knows is different. And knowledge, just like everything in our daily life, changes with time. That is why what the Good Fisherman knows almost does not fit in with modern times, as they call it. To me, more than anything else, it must be because Canchero and his kind have nearly destroyed all the fish; and without fish, how can one be a fisherman? Still, one learns by seeing, listening, living.

That's how it is, Alejandro. And it is worth remembering that many times we go against what we know, against what our heart tells us. Like what happened to me with the twins: Why did I stay that time, knowing it was not a good idea? Strange, isn't it? That is why at times I think that everything in life is as it should be, that we waste our time trying to escape from the hook that is destiny, that it is better to look at the world with old eyes and to live for the moment. . . . I wonder . . . Perhaps that is the only way to understand don Franco, for example. Remember him? He was the best director the barriada schools ever had.

He was a good teacher. He had patience. You must remember that you used to needle him with your articles in *La Antorcha*, that rag you used to publish and sell in the markets: "Run for mayor, don Franco, do it for Villa María." . . . He did not listen to you for a long time, but in the end, even knowing that it was not a good idea, he got involved in politics. That was after you had gone off to the highlands, but before all of what terrorism brought suffocated us.

As I already told you, we never liked politicians. When the candidates would come, full of words, with their shifty eyes, we listened to them with our heads down so they would not hear our curses. But we had to go anyway because if we did not, when they ended up elected, they would not even come back, and our schools would suffer. . . . But, in any case, a short time after you visited us dressed like a woman—that would have been '85, right?—the government required us to vote. The fine was high. So we went to the polls and "let our fingers be stained with indelible ink," as they say. That was when we elected don Franco.

But let us backtrack a little, Alejandro; we still have time. After you left, don Franco still continued as he had been. He was teaching different things in various schools: about the earth, the past, numbers, languages, even about Los Gentiles, they say. He knew more than most. He walked through the streets of Villa María with his black suit, as if in mourning, talking with parents, chasing after those who had skipped school. Thanks to him, Viroca finished high school; they say that the mischievous boy had wanted to escape to Ecuador. Don Franco listened to everyone. He gave advice. He knew who could and who could not buy uniforms. He knew who drank too much and who did not. He would go right into their houses and pull them out by the ears. He took the graduating classes on trips to walk in El Dorado, "so they can learn who they are," he said. I think that he walked with Los Gentiles because when he came to defend La Piedra, all dressed in black, he sat at a distance holding in his hands a stick, also black, not saying anything. His mere presence gave people courage.

He must have heard your words, full of accusations, provocations. Many times people do not listen when they hear, but only later, when the words echo in the mind like waves against internal rocks—days, months, years later. . . . I wonder . . . maybe he was tired of letting others govern Chimbote, like you used to say. Genaro says that, actually, don Franco got tired of asking for chalk and getting maps of Europe, as they call it; once they even sent him a skeleton of a gorilla for him to teach about humans. Isn't that something? Genaro sometimes sees everything as a joke. I wonder if he has arrived yet. He always moves only when he wants to. . . .

One day in June, when the leaders of don Franco's party gathered in the Plaza de Armas to sing the praises of the government, all of a sudden, just like Viroca, don Franco made an announcement—that he was going to run for mayor. His enemies were finally happy. At last he had become like them. Of course, some people in Villa María were hopeful. They thought that don Franco would be able to resist the slime of Canchero and his kind. But most of us resigned ourselves to sadness. We knew not only that we were losing a good teacher, but that we were going to see him ruined, corrupted. Not even Los Gentiles could save him.

As with all things new, at first everything was going well. Don Franco talked about making changes: that tax revenues should stay in Chimbote, that laborers should enjoy job security, that there should be more hospitals built, that we should have electricity. . . . But it was as if by merely saying those words, he thought his promises had been fulfilled. He did not manage to do anything. Quite the opposite. Within a year he became a millionaire. He bought himself several fishing boats and two houses, and he spent his final days in Trujillo, that city that wants to be like Lima. In time, he suffered from his ill-gotten wealth. He became just skin and bones. He never came back to Villa María. He must have been ashamed to see us. Just as well.

Poor don Franco. Even knowing that Canchero was soiling everything, he still got into politics. He tried to do the impossible. He swam against the current. Canchero was still at the height of his power in those days. He had everything: boats, factories, whore houses, policemen, politicians, informers, markets, soccer teams, cinemas, even shoe stores. . . . But everything was about to change. Genaro told you that when you came to take refuge in Tancay, dressed like a woman, with Canchero at your heels: "He is about to fall," he told you. "Others want to eat. But he is being true to the evil he carries inside him. He thinks he is invincible." You probably did not listen to him.

But cursed be fate! Things have not gotten better. Others have taken his place. And now it is even worse. What is in control now is no longer people, but duendes, nylon nets, naked power, sheer money, evil without hatred. Because, in spite of everything, Canchero would at least still go into bars and whore houses like an old tramboyo. His wickedness could be read in his face. With his death, the power of Capital, as they call it, has only grown. Now it seems that even the sea is dying without knowing who is killing it.

29
La Cabra

Yes, it seems like the world is changing, Alejandro. People no longer believe in the whims of Los Gentiles or that maybe everything in the world is as it should be, that there is a design for even the way we dry our tears. And maybe they are right. It all depends on how one sees things. Even a Good Fisherman will not just sit all day and later say that it was predetermined that he not catch a single fish. The Good Fisherman also does not expect much from luck. He makes his own luck. But making your own luck is not the same as doing things against their nature. When the damn factories killed all the fish, the Good Fisherman could not catch anything, with luck or without it. Do you understand? Everything has its own way of being. And, as I was telling you, sometimes we do not get the meaning of the nature of things until long after we have lived them. That is what happened in the case of Father Parker and La Cabra, for example.

In the summer of 1968—a month before Canchero chased you away for the first time, but long before you came back dressed as a woman—in one of those summers when even shadows hide, the people of Villa María had a meeting to discuss the case of La Cabra, that woman of the night who had a bar on the Pan American Highway. You must remember her because you spent several nights there. Don't get uncomfortable, Alejandro. I, too, was young once. We are just remembering, that is all. . . .

After a lot of complaints, the Association of Parents of Families demanded that she come forth to defend herself before the community. It was said that that was an old custom. Doña Pelagia assured us that it came from the time of the Chan Chan, that neither the Incas nor the Spaniards had been able to erase our custom of shouting out our truths in public. . . . I believe that it was, instead, one of doña Pelagia's own ideas, invented for the occasion, something to resolve a problem that seemed to have no remedy. Because doña Pelagia really does not like to take credit for things, even though she has done a lot for the people. . . .

Anyway, the news spread through the desert like a mudslide in winter. Many arrived at the school before dawn to find the best seats. There they waited, seated at the student desks like school children, until doña Eva, La Cabra, arrived. She came wearing a short yellow dress with wide sleeves. She looked like a butterfly from the marshes. She carried her black patent leather shoes in her hands and twirled them in front of her as if to fan herself. She seemed very distracted. But that was not it at all. Without anybody asking her, she complained, so everyone could hear, that she had been dancing all night and that her calluses were killing her.

The people whispered and stretched their necks to get a better look at her. La Cabra then walked slowly, with much flourish, to the little table at the front of the hall. From there she looked at the people like a hawk at her prey and sat down crossing her legs just like a man. With that gesture she silenced everyone. When the silence seemed about to bring down the reed-mat walls, La Cabra began to speak. She had a deep voice, raspy, like a goose.

She said that she was tired of people calling her names. That she was not just some ordinary woman of the night. That, like everyone else, she had a good mother. That she had come only because she wanted to. . . . Then she raised her finger, pointed to several men at her feet, all seated at the little student desks, and she dared them to prohibit her from earning a living. And before anyone could say anything, she got up from her chair and began to pace. She went back and forth in front of the people, swaying like a junco in bloom.

It was clear that the men there were no match for La Cabra. And there was not a single woman who might be able to stop her. I am sure that this was something that doña Pelagia had not anticipated. And do not even ask me why doña Pelagia herself was not there. I gave up a long time ago trying to grasp the full meaning of what she says and does. . . . And so La Cabra continued, even more brazen: "How can you call me names, damn it! Just to show you, I'm going to build an even bigger bar. I came only so that you could see me and that I could see you in broad daylight. I'm not afraid of anyone. I've got you all by the balls!" That is how she spoke, with her fist in the air. She was a tough woman.

The sunlight filtering through the roof of reed mats seemed more golden than ever. A sound like a swarm of horseflies was rising in the corners. The people did not know what to do. And then, when La Cabra seemed to have command of everyone, the low, whimpering voice of a peasant woman was heard. She had been far from everything, way in the back, leaning against the reed-mat walls, with her basket of fruit. She spoke strangely. But it was understood that she had not seen with her own eyes what went on in La Cabra's bar, but that, like everyone else present there, she could well imagine. She said that La Cabra was giving a bad example to the children: "How many sons and daughters go to sleep hungry because their fathers spend their paycheck at your bar? How many women go over to wait for their husbands at your door?"

La Cabra saw the woman among the men and stood squarely, with her hands on her hips. She let her speak a little longer before interrupting her to make it clear to her that none of that was her fault, that perhaps the peasant was not woman enough to keep a man faithful. . . . Now there was dead silence—a silence that announces that something is about to happen, but you don't know what. Everybody turned around to get a better look at whoever had spoken from the back. For her part, the peasant woman got up from her place, brushed off her skirt, and began to walk toward La Cabra with small steps, speaking in Quechua. Her mysterious words fluttered in the dead silence.

When the peasant woman got up to La Cabra's side, without waiting a second she gave her two slaps in the face that made the little school's reed-mat walls shake. Slap! Slap! Damn. It seemed like the ringing of the blows would last all day. Then, before anyone could react, the two women knocked each other down. La Cabra's shoes went flying. Her butterfly dress appeared and disappeared in the dust and the sand. They pushed. They panted. Until one of the walls tumbled down because La Cabra had grabbed the peasant woman by her braids and was spinning her around like a top. Then, finally, the men intervened. It took six strong men to separate them. But by then there was blood on that desert.

The news of the fight spread throughout the valley. People repeated the story in ever more creative ways. Sadly for the other women, in all the gossip it was said that La Cabra won not only the fight, but also the right to stay in Villa María. So in order to provide for clientele who now came from as far away as Lima, La Cabra had to enlarge her establishment and contract more women of the night. The men swarmed around there like mojarrillas on an old pier. Worse yet: as if to rub salt in an open wound, La Cabra had a huge sign painted for her new establishment: The Balls of La Cabra. The letters were in red . . .

But, as we have seen, everything has its limit. And so that story could not end like that. In the long run, La Cabra's victory came to embitter our hearts even more because in her sad fall she exacted a high price from the one who put an end to her exploits: Father Parker.

30
Father Parker

They have stopped murmuring. You can hear the wind. . . . Sometimes people talk from sheer nervousness. . . . Doña Pelagia must have calmed their spirits, with her way of being . . . or, maybe, they are listening to us. Because I am sure that many of those who are in the little parlor remember very clearly what happened. . . . Do you think that is why doña Pelagia made us remember in this little backyard in the open air, so that everyone would see how we weave common memories? We have no choice now but to please them and go on with the story. What do you say? My body is not hurting much anymore. Besides, the story of La Cabra and Father Parker has been so woven into our past that it is now better to bring it out into the light. . . .

On another day of blinding heat—this must have been around '69 because I remember that, thank God, the days of '68 had already passed, and people could walk in the streets in the middle of the day—Father Parker came to Villa María to show the medical outpost to a gringa from Ireland, as they call it—a gringa who went around everywhere with a yellow flyswatter and who had come as a nurse to replace Sister Josefa. . . . Remember that in those days there was still no hospital in those deserts. . . . Anyway, Father Parker took advantage of his visit to listen to the complaints of his faithful. And, of course, among so many bad thoughts to chase away and so many souls to help get into heaven, he heard about La Cabra.

By itself, that complaint was not too serious. Father Parker was an understanding man when it came to the people's flaws, and he could have heard any confession without bitterness in his heart. It is just a Peruvian thing, he would have said. But, as doña Pelagia says, things never stay simple when they can become complicated. It so happened that for nearly three years now the poor father had been yelling and screaming for them to close La Casa Rosada, the brothel that was near his parish church. But since bad habits are as persistent as waves, there was nothing he could do.

Every Sunday morning shortly before mass, the women of the night would pass by, swaying like juncos in bloom, from La Casa Rosada to the Pan American Highway. They would gather at the colectivo stop that was right in front of the church's main door to pinch each other, to kiss each other, to laugh, until they took their colectivo to La Caleta Hospital to be examined by a doctor. Because in those days those women had better health care than all of us put together. . . . In any case, poor Father Parker had learned in time to forgive them. When he saw them pinching each other, he would go the other way.

It seems that what put the whole thing in a totally different light, what Father Parker could not possibly ignore, was that in all the yelling in the fight with the men who held her down, La Cabra had said—with a feeling that almost pierced the eardrums of the souls of the devout women when they heard it—that she would shit on the Son, on the Father, and on the Most Blessed Virgin.

One by one, the devout women of Villa María burdened the poor father with their fear, their bitterness. One by one, they asked for comfort for their souls. So that, little by little, on that blindingly hot day in '69, Father Parker was pressured by the fear of his faithful, by the vision of women passing by the door of his church like juncos in bloom, by his anger at that sinful life coiled up in his gut ever since he set foot on Peruvian soil. And finally, when the church bells of Villa María rang out at twelve o'clock, Father Parker closed his confessional, put on the cassock that he never used because he was a gringo, and set out for Las Bolas de La Cabra.

As you may remember, Father Parker was tall and brawny. Genaro says that someone told him that when the priest was young, he had played football back home. Not the football that we play, but the one where players throw themselves at their opponents looking to knock them out. It's for tough men, they say. Of course, when he

124

arrived here, he was already a little paunchy, but you could still see his former self. . . . In any case, on that midday of blinding heat, his face red like a tomato, his steps long and heavy, his cassock and his eyes black like a buzzard gave him the air of a warrior looking for a fight. Something had to happen.

As he walked toward Las Bolas de La Cabra, the gossip about his anger spread throughout Villa María. The children got out of his way, and an army of angry women grew behind him. When Father Parker arrived at Las Bolas de La Cabra, there was so much dust that even the people at Tancay knew that something was happening in Villa María. Imagine that. Chochita told me later that the fishermen climbed to the top of the stout mountain to see what was happening, but it was so hot they could see only a trembling horizon.

When Father Parker arrived, he paused for a moment in front of La Cabra's red door, took a deep breath, made the sign of the cross, and with a single blow broke it down. The devout women followed him inside, like ants. In the blink of an eye they turned everything upside down. La Cabra went out into the street in her underwear, covering herself with a white sheet. Some say that the women found several men sleeping inside. Others say that they found only La Cabra and don Carpio, a man from the jungle who was her lover. Who knows? The fact is that Father Parker chased La Cabra into the street, shouting at her, hurling strange words at her. La Cabra only covered herself with the sheet, full of shame. . . . It is possible that La Cabra would not have done what she did that day if Father Parker had let her go when she was already an orphan in the street. But by now the priest had a very unclean heart. He forgot himself. As if possessed by hidden forces, he pointed his finger at her and told her that she was a blasphemous woman.

La Cabra felt that word like a heavy blow on the back of her neck. She crumbled; she curled up on the sand. From there she heard Father Parker repeat the word a thousand times, as the devout women surrounded her. I think La Cabra did not know what it was to be a blasphemous woman. Not even I knew until it was explained to me by my Aurora, who asked Sister Josefa when she came to Villa María for the last time. La Cabra probably thought it was a curse.

Each time Father Parker called her blasphemous, she would tremble and cry more.

Now it is clear that Father Parker used the word too much. That is what happens when one has an unclean heart. One no longer considers the consequences. After La Cabra had cried and trembled enough, she got up from the ground, traced a circle in the sand with her left foot, stood in its center, and said for all to hear: "In this circle of Los Gentiles I curse you. With this heart I guarantee it: you will die of an illness that no one will understand. You will die with a dry and bitter heart. With your last breath you will remember me."

If Father Parker had been any other man, the women who surrounded La Cabra would have trembled to hear that curse. Because, in that moment of sheer fury, when La Cabra invoked Los Gentiles, she surrendered herself to them completely. But since it concerned Father Parker, a priest from the United States, as they call it, the women did not even feel the thorn that La Cabra had planted in their hearts. Only many years later, when the devout women of Villa María received the news that the priest had died, half crazy, bleating like a goat, talking about Chimbote in his sleep, did they realize that Los Gentiles had heard La Cabra in her moment of pain. But that was long after the earthquake. Father Parker was still here when the shaking came.

31
One Life for Another

When the earthquake shook Chimbote, Father Parker was lecturing to the students of Mundo Mejor High School. As you probably remember, the school had just recently been built. Its walls looked like mirrors of different colors that had bloomed overnight right out of the desert. They say that many of its students turned out really well, that one even became a senator. . . . But, anyway. When the students felt the tell-tale humming in the ground and in the air, they ran looking for a way out. They rushed however they could toward the front door.

In the middle of all that rattling Father Parker noticed that the archway over the door was coming down, that the students were not going to be able to get out. So, with the agility of a cat, the priest ran to the door, opened it halfway with one pull, and put his shoulder against it. He held the door like that, by sheer force, until the last disoriented child ran out. . . . And when the earth decided to calm down, Father Parker was still at his post, covered with dust. He had lost his eyeglasses. His feet, his arms, his face were covered with blood.

One never knows about people, Alejandro. They often seem to be what they are not, but it is also true that sometimes experiences change us. The thing is that the fright was too much for Father Parker's soul, in spite of the good deed he had just done. That is why, when the last tremor passed, the poor father started to walk alone amidst the ruins of his school. They say he seemed like a different man, with a deep sadness pooled in his eyes. He had even lost the desire to talk to people. He did not even respond to greetings. He would just walk around the ruins, talking to himself and pointing out the broken things to someone not there.

He stayed like that for a long time, until, seeing that the priest was not getting any better, in spite of the masses and in spite of the fact that the colorful walls of Mundo Mejor were being raised up again, the pope himself, they say, asked him to return to his homeland to rest. Since Father Parker was a good priest, he obeyed. But I am sure it must have cost him a lot to accept the fact that he would leave Chimbote forever. Don't you think so, Alejandro? Maybe he remembered La Cabra and could foresee his destiny. . . . The thing is that when the students asked that a final mass be said in his honor, people came from all over the valley to bid him farewell. There was a lot of weeping.

For several years afterwards, each time a new priest would come to Chimbote, almost all of them from a port in the United States called Baltimore, the women who had followed Father Parker to chase away sins that day in '69 would ask about him: how he was, if he was talking yet, if he remembered them. No one gave them any news. Until Sister Josefa wrote to I-don't-know-who, saying that Father Parker was in an asylum. Genaro says that in the land of the gringos there are many places where they put people who go crazy from thinking so much about their money and worrying so much about futures, as they say, and that the best of those places are called asylums. I wonder . . . but, in any case, Sister Josefa said in her letter that Father Parker did not recognize anyone anymore and that he passed the time repeating strange words to himself. . . .

What happened was that his heart was drying up. That is the only reason why men end their lives that way. Because, though you may not believe it, Alejandro, even the pain that anguish brings gives us reason to go on living. As long as the heart does not dry up, there is hope. Poor Father Parker: he must have died in some place with a dried-up heart. From nostalgia perhaps. Because I know that he liked the desert. Villa María. The children. The thing is that he used the power of words too much. Genaro says that he must have died with no memory either. Because La Cabra asked that he remember her. That means that at the hour of his death the poor father must have seen only the bitter face of vengeance.

La Cabra disappeared from the time they threw her out of her house. No one ever heard any more about her. Doña Pelagia says that the price La Cabra paid for making that curse was heavy: her beauty. She says that at the same time that Father Parker was dying of an endless nostalgia in those faraway lands, La Cabra was becoming wrinkled with old age. She says they most likely died at the same time, trying to forgive each other from afar. That is how curses are when Los Gentiles are involved. To get something, you have to give something of equal value. In this case it was one life for another.

32
The Omens

Well, Alejandro, we are now coming to the end. We have walked a lot. We have gone as far away as Lurigancho and Baltimore, as they call it. We have walked to the very edges of misfortune. . . . There is nothing more to do now but to return to the rocks. We must remember the ending. Even if it pains our souls. Even if we have to close our wounds and thus run the risk of forgetfulness. . . .

Tancay truly began to die in the late '80s. When you visited us, things were already going bad. Didn't you notice? Maybe not, because you must have been preoccupied with your own thorns. . . . Half of the fishermen had already gone. There was not a single crabber left. The mussels were coming loose from the rocks and floating like charcoal in water. . . . But, to tell you the truth, the bad omens began much earlier.

The first bad omen occurred shortly after the mudslide that was a gift from the earthquake of '70. One day the sea was completely red at dawn. Not the red of August, when the sun is sinking and paints everything like a wave without sound. Not the red that announces the death of someone very special. No. A blood red. A red that stuck to the rocks, to the mussels, to the hands. The poor ducks did not know what to do. Now they would not even dive. The little sea lions would look at us from below with their little faces all streaked with red. When Genaro saw the poor things like that, all disoriented, he wept. He nearly threw himself from La Pared out of sheer rage.

The second bad omen occurred several months later, still in the '70s. Do you remember the blue flies that followed us all over the place when we did not have a market yet? Well, when don Augusto traced the lines in the desert, they had no other recourse than to go and live in the marshes of Veintisiete de Octubre. That is where they must have settled in, together with the dragonflies. Because there are dragonflies of every size and color in those marshes. But then, after the mudslide, there appeared overnight mosquitoes that looked like dragonflies—except that they were the color of straw. Where could they have come from? Nobody knew. Doña Pelagia says that they just woke up, that the mosquitoes had been sleeping around here since the time of the Chan Chan. . . . Who knows? The thing is that one day they were buzzing around at dawn all over the place. The children tried to corner them to catch them with their hands.

At first they were content to buzz around in the streets on sunny afternoons. At nightfall they would go back to sleep with the toads in the marshes. However, ever since the mosquitoes appeared, the people who walked by Veintisiete de Octubre noticed that the marshes were growing quiet. Not even the giant toads were making noise anymore. A heavy silence was growing in the warm waters.

By January of '72, when the heat would not let us sleep, the mosquitoes became so brazen that they began to suck blood from people in broad daylight. They showed up just about anywhere. They appeared in our soup and in our underwear. Since there was no breeze, they floated like a thick cloud over Villa María. The people had to walk around with bundles of rue or eucalyptus to defend themselves. Seeing all that, doña Pelagia told us that things were going from bad to worse in the valley, that the forces of hatred and evil were joining together once again.

The third bad omen occurred in the '80s. The currents of El Niño brought heavy rains for the first time since God knows when. The roofs could not withstand it, and the people had to let the water take over everything. When the heavy rainfall stopped, the days became extremely humid. A dark and thick mist like the smell of death covered everything. The sun was lost for days. When the sun returned in force and dispelled the smell, dawn found the desert green and covered with flowers. Travelers stopped their buses and colectivos on the Pan American Highway to see the living blanket that seemed to float over the desert. Aside from all the celebration, doña Pelagia warned us that the forces of hatred were gaining strength.

The people who remained in Villa María after the tidal wave saw all these occurrences as omens of a grave disaster. The old folks like me peered into the wind, fearing hurricanes. But the truth was that none of us knew what hurricanes were. Father Parker and don Franco had already left for other places. There was no one to trust, no one to ask. Then the rumor went around that hurricanes were like landslides, only in reverse: a rainfall with winds so strong that they could carry donkeys and houses all the way up to the highlands.

The people seemed dazed in those days, Alejandro. We moved in a haze of uncertain fear. Strange things had been happening already for many months. Until one day, when dawn broke with a red sun, a thick, gray, slimy fog came and settled in the streets. The sun and the wind seemed to give up. That was the last straw for the people. We gathered in front of the church to request special masses. Seeing the fear on our faces, Father O'Hara, who had replaced Father Parker, granted our request.

So much for masses! The fog would not clear up. People had to go around talking out loud so they would not bump into each other. Cars would go around with their horns blowing at all hours. Roosters became hoarse from sounding the alarm so often. . . . Things could not go on like that . . . so doña Pelagia advised us to make a pilgrimage to the great apu who watches over the valley. "Just go, without asking for anything. It is not necessary," she told us. No sooner said than done. As if by magic, the fog lifted. The next day Father O'Hara climbed up the mountain carrying a cross. "Miracles should be shared," he said. To this day, doña Pelagia makes the sign of the cross every time she thinks about those days.

There were other smaller signs. . . . Viewed from hindsight, much of what happened in the valley since the earthquake was an omen of the disaster that would come. Genaro insists that even the death of Canchero was a bad omen. . . . Of course, doña Pelagia never tired of warning us. . . . We did not listen to her. But what could we have done anyway?

Since we are remembering from the beginning, it is worth saying

133

that when you went to the highlands and the police came to search our houses, our backyards, our pots and pans, doña Pelagia told us that all of that was transitory, that the worst was yet to come. We did not listen to her—even though Villa María was already half smothered by mudslides, earthquakes, floods, mosquitoes, and the damn smell of boiled fish that would not even let us eat. . . . It must be that when terror comes with a human face, the horrors that the world brings us seem small.

33
Canchero

As I was telling you, Genaro says that the death of Canchero put an end to a phase in our lives; that in that instant evil shed its human name and face; that from then on power would exist naked, metallic, plastic, without color, without odor, without pain, and without hatred. Perhaps this is true. . . .

The truth is that it was a strange death. Canchero was at the peak of his power. He owned everything. He went everywhere with an open shirt, baring his chest adorned with gold medals. He used to challenge the pimps at La Casa Rosada with his knife. He knew everything about everyone. He intimidated everybody. Government officials would come to grovel before him for the feast of San Pedro. One time he insisted that they play soccer in the Plaza de Armas. He would embarrass them that way. He would undermine their spirits, their authority. But, as I was telling you, Canchero crossed the line. Because doña Pelagia is right: even evil has its limits.

He had a relationship with a tall, attractive prostitute known as La Argentina who lived at La Casa Rosada. She was his partner in vice, let us say. He used to drive her around town in an open car, attended by a boy with earrings. The poor skinny kid spent his days shooing the flies away from her and protecting her from the dust.

One night, it must have been in January of 1986, shortly after you left for the highlands, Canchero showed up at La Casa Rosada. As always, he seemed bent on spreading his vice and his rage. . . . As soon as he arrived, he ordered the boy with the earrings to bar the door of La Argentina's room and not let her out. "Tonight I'm going to have La Giganta," they say he said. La Giganta was a woman from Pataz, this small. She looked like a little doll.

He began drinking and spraying the floor with champagne. As if well paid, they all came out to fawn over him. They all made room for him. La Giganta felt special. She drank like a man, they say. But after several hours La Giganta could not take any more. . . . She was very small. . . . She sat down in a corner and passed out. Then Canchero, as if he had gone mad, grabbed her by the scruff of the neck and bathed her with champagne. He wanted to drown her, they say.

At that moment, César Pañuelos, La Giganta's lover, jumped in to defend her. With one slap Canchero sent him spinning. In all her drunkenness, seeing her lover on the floor, La Giganta rose up like a cat and climbed on top of Canchero. The old tramboyo staggered around the room with La Giganta on his back, holding onto him by the hair. "Come out and kill me, fags," said Canchero, as if calling out invisible pimps. "Come out and kill me, if you can." The customers pretended not to hear anything. They let him shout like a madman.

But he was not crazy. Quite the opposite. Someone had already barred the main door of La Casa Rosada. The music from the loudspeakers kept repeating without anybody changing the record. Then several strangers appeared from rooms and hallways. The regular customers scampered in fear into the little private rooms. They say that Canchero started to reach for the dagger that he always carried with him, but before he could pull it out, he was disemboweled with curved knives. He fell down, with La Giganta and all.

Only then, seeing what was really happening, the midget sobered up and screamed bloody murder. But nobody lifted a finger to help Canchero, not even the whores who had praised him so much in life. It seems that even César Pañuelos was in on the conspiracy. . . . Poor Giganta. She did not know that she was complicit in the crime until the last moment. . . . They say that when Canchero was agonizing on the floor soaked with champagne, La Giganta was crying with rage, cursing everyone, and kissing his wounds. It must have been sad. . . .

Genaro says that Canchero knew they were going to kill him,

that he was ready to face death when he entered La Casa Rosada, that he wanted to die as he had lived. Only he did not count on La Giganta climbing on his back like a duende. . . . His death, says Genaro, shed light on the human side of power because, in the end, Canchero did something that nobody expected of him: he saved La Argentina's life. Because Genaro swears that that woman would have slit her throat for him. . . . Perhaps they loved each other. . . .

When they buried him, La Argentina followed the cortege from far behind. She walked straight and tall, dressed in white, consoling the boy with the earrings. After the burial, she closed herself up in La Casa Rosada and did not come out for years. The people said that in her very own way she had become a nun. . . .

Not long ago the priests of Mundo Mejor managed to erase finally the last vestiges of the brothel. Doña Pelagia says that she saw La Argentina leaving Chimbote in the middle of the night. She was still accompanied by the boy with the earrings. But now she also had a little boy by the hand.

34
The Disaster

The mojarrillas disappeared first. Imagine that. Despite the fact that they would feed on anything. Shortly after that the tramboyos abandoned their holes and came out to splash around in the whirlpools. The chitas were finished last. Maybe it was because they would feed farther out, beyond the black mussels. The *pardelas* stopped flying. The pelicans got lost in the distances. . . . Only the ghost crabs went on stubbornly cleaning the beach. They multiplied. They worked day and night. But they could not keep up with the waste, with death.

When I saw that the destruction was not going to stop, I told the men that it was time to leave that sitio. Poor things. Some did not know what to do. They would walk around and around those rocks, with hope in their eyes. But everything was useless. The water was too dirty. . . . That slow death lasted for months . . . until, one night in winter, Genaro came looking for me. "We have to go to the beach," he told me. "It seems like everything is going to hell." He was obviously in despair; because he never liked to curse like that.

When we crossed the desert and arrived at Tancay, we found about a hundred beached sea lions. There were also turtles, crabs, *cachemas*, sand sharks and deep sea sharks, tramboyos, blowfish, manta rays, *merluzas*, even pejeblancos—all of them splashing at the water's edge, trying to save themselves from the yellowish water. . . . In the light of the full moon, almost blue, like this one, it was a sight that gave us chills. . . .

So Genaro took me by the arm and brought me along those paths he knows. . . . A thick film like a dark veil undulated over the waves. The poor waves were mute, subdued. We climbed to La Pared and found that even in that temple of Los Gentiles, the sea had the silence of death. We wept with rage, Alejandro. Even in death, it seemed, Canchero was pissing on everything. His vomit was still pouring out. . . .

That is how it was, Alejandro. On that full-moon night we could see the smoke from the factories. Far away. Far away . . . and there, for a moment that seemed endless, we felt abandoned by Los Gentiles. We were angry with them because they did not want to fight. Always retreating. Farther and farther away. . . since the beginning. . . . We even remembered that you might be up in the highlands searching for justice, as you said. We remembered you and said that only those who are like you would be saved, that you had run away. . . . Our hearts were not clean, Alejandro. We sinned. We were selfish. Forgive us. In our hearts we knew that nothing good was in store for you.

From that night on I did not go to Tancay anymore. I went back only yesterday. When you returned for the last time. The sea was red as of old, and my wrinkles had multiplied.

35
The Rainbow

The cemetery in Chimbote is new. The wind blows low there, and the winter mist is white, almost transparent. Genaro says that it is an oasis in time. It must be. The good thing is that it is difficult to get lost in its labyrinths. One can see the crosses of loved ones from far away.

Doña Pelagia says that before we arrived, there were cemeteries scattered everywhere. When Chimbote grew, the politicians came up with the idea of gathering all Las Almitas in one place. The poor things must have suffered a lot with the transfer. Doña Pelagia says that people started dreaming awake for many days. They would see Las Almitas walking in the streets, skin and bones, using the dust like a shield.

The people protested. There were strikes. Demonstrations. But the four policemen they had back then broke them up with sticks, and the priests announced that God loved all the dead, even if they changed sitios. "Then why bury them in cemeteries? Why put little crosses or little mounds of black earth? Why plant little flowers for them?" said the people. It did not help. . . . Since then, our loved ones have rested at the foot of the yellowish gray mountain. They will not move from there anymore. There are too many of them now.

The cemetery is surrounded by a high wall made of straw and mud. I wonder who built it? No one knows anymore. The good thing is that it is not affected by the sun or by earthquakes. In the earthquake of '70, for example, it did not get even a single crack. The rains that came with El Niño ran off it just like water on glass. It must have been descendants from the Chan Chan, perhaps. . . .

It has a beautiful entrance. A steel fence in the form of a rainbow holds letters, also of steel, that say "Rest." Doña Pelagia says that it was a gift from Canchero himself, from when he controlled the steel mill, the Pittsburgh, as they call it. Who knows? Maybe Canchero knew that he would end up resting forever behind that wall, in some ordinary grave, with no flowers or anything. Because not even La Argentina comes to clean his sitio. . . .

Women dressed in black sell flowers at the entrance. Don't be startled when you see their eyes the color of ash. It is not because of anything serious. It is that, in spite of time and experience, they cannot bear the pain of farewells. They hardly ever sleep. And do not be startled also by their constant sighs. It's just that, from being in that sitio for so long, they have forgotten how to breathe. That is why they speak so softly, as if murmuring. It is not because they keep secrets. . . .

Look how the night has become, Alejandro. Dark. The stars have gone. It seems as if the shadows know when the spirit is weakening. . . . Here comes doña Pelagia, with candles and friends. Do not resist their weeping, Alejandro. Do not run away from their pain. Set yourself softly inside them, instead. Nestle in them. . . . Tomorrow we will bury you.

36
At the Cemetery

Alejandro Moscoso Huamán. You arrived in Villa María in 1966. You got close to us, the humble folks of Tancay. As best we could, we tried to show you our world. "Like this, Alejandro." "That way, Alejandro." . . . Don Morales, who is present here, tried very hard. . . . But you had eyes and heart for other things. . . . You organized the people. You wrote in your newspaper. You were good at that . . . until you left for the highlands. In search of justice, you said. . . .

You came back later. With fear in your eyes. Disguised as a woman. Fleeing from the terror that was growing bigger day by day everywhere. . . . Maybe you were a terrorist, as they call them. Maybe you turned bad, as they say. We do not know. We do not want to know. . . .

You left again. For a long time . . . until you came back for the last time, the day before yesterday. . . . They had covered your head with a black sack. Your chest was naked and slashed. . . . From where must they have brought you . . . ? They threw you into the sea. So that no one would bury you, they must have said. So that no one would know about you. . . . But we found you. Washed ashore like the sea lions, the fish, the crabs, the merluzas. . . . The omens, it seems, are proving true. . . . The misfortune is growing in our valley. . . . We have no other recourse but to have courage.

I, Pelagia Salvatierra Moche, am present here. I plead guilty for having washed your wounds. . . . Don Morales, at my side, pleads guilty for having sat and remembered with you. . . . Don Genaro, in the back, pleads guilty for having called your name out loud three times. All of us here present, your people, plead guilty for having brought you little candles, flowers, and other offerings. . . .

We will remember your name, Alejandro. We will keep coming to clean your sitio. Nestle in it. Feel the mystery of its nature, of its way of being, so that one day you can find your path and return to dance with the sun. . . .

Glossary

Even though the Spanish terms retained in this translation can be understood in context or are explained within the text, the following glossary might be helpful to the reader.

aguaje	Contaminated ocean waters, sludge
almita	Ghost, spirit; diminutive or endearing form of *alma*
apu	Mountain god
barriada	Shantytown
bola	Ball
bolichero	One who fishes with nets
borde	Fringe, edge, border
borracho	Gray gurnard, a fish of northern Peruvian waters
caballito de totora	Small canoe made of rushes
cabra	Goat
cachema	Peruvian weakfish
caito	Tool used for catching *maruchas*
cangrejero	One who catches crabs *(cangrejos)*
ceviche	Dish made of fresh fish marinated in lime juice, hot peppers, and onions
chicha	A Peruvian beer made from corn or peanuts
chita	Grunt fish
chitero	One who catches *chita*
cocho	Brown pelican
colectivo	Communal taxi
colorado	Reddish

cordelero	One who works with rope or cord, or, in this case, fishing line
duende	Sprite, pixie, elf, ghost
El Patillo Ahogado	The Drowned Duckling
El Pozo	The Well
gentiles	Spirits and gods of pre-Colombian people
gringo	Fair-skinned person
guanaco	A wild Andean ruminant, related to the llama and alpaca
huaco	Pre-Colombian ceramic pottery
huaico	Mudslide
huayno	A popular Andean music and dance
junco	Rush plant
La Casa Rosada	The Pink House
La Cocina	The Kitchen
La Mesa	The Table
langostino	A small crustacean, similar to crayfish
La Pared	The Wall
La Piedra	The Rock
La Playa de los Chungos	The Beach of Smooth Stones
La Playa del Viento	The Windy Beach
La Playa Desierta	The Deserted Beach
La Punta	The Point
Las Dos Hermanas	The Two Sisters
lenguado	Flounder
marucha	Very small clam, commonly used for bait
merluza	Hake
miñoca	Saltwater worm, commonly used for bait
mojarrilla	Croaker

mojarrillero	One who catches *mojarrilla*
nocturno	Nocturnal
palabra	Word
pampanito	Short-finned butterfish
pardela	Sea bird similar to a gull
pejeblanco	Goldeneye tilefish
pescador	Fisherman
Quechua	Language of the Inca people
retama	Low-growing bush with yellow flowers
rey	King
rocanrolero	Rock-and-roll singer
roseta	Four fishing hooks tied together in the form of a rose to fish without bait
rosetero	One who fishes with a *roseta*
sitio	Place, spot, location
tondero	A type of popular Afro-Peruvian music
totora	A type of rush plant that grows in marshes; used to make canoes
tramboyo	Blenny (fish)
vicuña	A wild Andean ruminant, related to the llama and alpaca
viña	Highfin king croaker

About the Author and Translator

Braulio Muñoz was born in Peru. Before coming to America, he was a stage actor, political leader, and radio and print journalist. He holds a Ph.D. in sociology from the University of Pennsylvania and has taught at various East Coast universities. He is currently Centennial Professor of Sociology at Swarthmore College. Professor Muñoz has written books and articles on sociology, psychology, philosophy, and literary criticism. *A Storyteller: Mario Vargas Llosa Between Civilization and Barbarism* (2000) is his most recent book on literary criticism. Professor Muñoz has also written works of fiction in English and Spanish. His first novel in English, *The Peruvian Notebooks*, was published by the University of Arizona Press (2006). *Alejandro and the Fishermen of Tancay* is the translation of his first novel in Spanish, *Alejandro y los pescadores de Tancay*, published in Italy in 2004. Professor Muñoz travels frequently to lecture in several languages throughout Europe and Latin America. He is currently teaching courses on social and critical theory at Swarthmore College and is working on a book on social theory as well as on a new novel in Spanish.

Nancy K. Muñoz (née Bailey) was born in Providence, Rhode Island. In 1967, she traveled to Chimbote, Peru, where she worked as a nurse setting up medical posts among the poor. During that time, she met and married Braulio Muñoz. Upon returning to the United States, she continued to work as a nurse, and she and Braulio returned to Peru regularly. In 1992, she translated his book *Sons of the Wind* into Spanish. *Alejandro and the Fishermen of Tancay* is her first translation from the Spanish. Nancy and Braulio have two children and three grandchildren. They live in Swarthmore, Pennsylvania.